DR. CAPPELETTI'S
CHORUS

DR. CAPPELETTI'S CHORUS

A Novel

by

GERARD R. D'ALESSIO

iUniverse LLC
Bloomington

Dr. Cappeletti's Chorus

iUniverse books may be ordered through booksellers or by contacting:

iUniverse LLC
1663 Liberty Drive
Bloomington, IN 47403
www.iuniverse.com
1-800-Authors (1-800-288-4677)

ISBN: 978-1-4917-0205-5 (sc)
ISBN: 978-1-4917-0206-2 (ebk)

Printed in the United States of America

iUniverse rev. date: 08/02/2013

This book is dedicated to my wife,
Susan K. D'Alessio

Dr. Cappeletti's Chorus

By

Gerard R. D'Alessio

Betty

Clarksburg, where I live now and where I have always lived, is a medium-sized city of a little more than fifty thousand people according to a recent census. We're located in the Allegheny Mountains of central Pennsylvania between the Susquehanna River on the south and Fairfax Mountain to the north. The river provided early transportation for logging and other commerce, and, later on, it gave the railroad access through the mountain range. The mountains and surrounding forests supplied the timber and coal on which the Clark family and other settlers back in the early 1800s made their fortunes. Its location insured Clarksburg's continuing ability to survive economically even after the timber ran out and it has always been a draw for immigrants looking for work. Recently, that has included a variety of Hispanics and Latinos, who have tended to settle in the older and poorer sections closer to the river.

Old City, with its warehouses, rooming houses, taverns and inns (and now: gift shops, ice-cream parlors, coffee shops and designer boutiques), nestles snugly against the river near the Market Street Bridge and the falls, and is bordered on its northern side by Clark Boulevard, which separates Old City from the rest of us in Clarksburg.

As the town grew, it spread, not only east and west along the river bank, but also northward to the foot of Fairfax Mountain. The original "millionaire's row," built by the timber barons, is at Twenty-Eighth Street. That was "the country" in the early and mid-1800s and thus safely removed from foreign laborers and the commerce and roughhouse of the waterfront. All the fancy homes built more recently are now much further north and west of the town center, up along High Street and Ridge Road. The new millionaire's row extends along Upper Mountain Avenue.

My house was left to me and my daughter when my husband died, and is closer to the center of town, on Tenth Street, just east of Market Street, which makes it convenient for me to take the bus downtown to the municipal building, the movie theater, shopping, and to my work at St. Joseph's Elementary School where I teach fifth grade.

I remember the first time I met Anthony Cappeletti. It was in early October of 1990 and I watched with a feeling of unease from behind my living room curtains as he helped my daughter into his car. He'd been polite and had smiled easily while we engaged in small talk as he waited for Laura to come downstairs. He was good looking, I'll give him that: tall and trim with that slick self-conscious smile so many Latin men have, and dark wavy hair a girl would kill for. My immediate impression was that he was a conceited, self-centered young man. I watched them drive away. A movie, they'd said. Well, how would I know? I remember thinking that I hoped that Laura would grow tired of him as she had of so many others. I probably had no need to worry that Laura would end up marrying an Italian boy, a son of a laborer. Of course I wanted more for her: a professional man for a husband and father to her children, as I myself had had. My Brian had been a teacher and then a principal until a heart attack struck him down in his prime. Laura should do at least as well. Son of an Italian laborer? Not if I had anything to do with it.

Laura was a freshman at Clarksburg State College then, and was doing very well. She was on an honor's scholarship program; as long as she maintained a 3.0 point grade average, she would continue to qualify for her full-tuition scholarship. Laura wasn't worried. She'd been the salutatorian in high school and wasn't having any trouble with her courses. She'd begun college with the idea of going into education like her father and I, but lately she was thinking of something else: maybe social work or the law. She didn't have that many electives in her first two years, and therefore had plenty of time to decide. In addition to her college courses, she worked as a salesgirl in one of the boutiques on Water Street three afternoons a week and she volunteered at St. Ignatius local hospital, on weekends. It was at the hospital, I learned, that she'd met Anthony.

He'd been waiting to take a discharged patient down to the main entrance and she'd been asked to carry the woman's overnight bag and a vase of flowers. He'd said hello and asked her name and made some pleasant small talk while they'd waited for the nurse to finish the paperwork. Then, after they'd helped the woman into a taxi, they'd talked some more before getting on with their duties. But, she knew then that he was interested. Later that day, he asked her if she wanted to go to the hospital cafeteria for a soda or something and she said yes. The following weekend, he asked her out. But, there was probably no need for me to worry. Laura was intelligent, mature, and ambitious. She wasn't going to settle for anything less than what she wanted. She was headstrong like her father, which translated into stubborn perseverance and dogged determination. No, no need to worry about Laura being distracted by some smooth-talker just because he had dark wavy hair and a self-satisfied smile. Although all of these thoughts had remained unspoken while I charmed him with my own easy Irish smile and played gracious hostess, my views—as if by telepathy—had been discerned by both my Laura and her young man.

Laura

"I don't think she likes me," Tony told me once we were in the car and driving to the cinema. Reflexively I turned quickly to him, ready to deny it. But I saw him smiling and knew he was all right with it. "Don't worry about it," I told him. "Mom has her set ways. She'll get over it. You'll see." I didn't have to spell out Mom's unreasonable prejudice (is there a reasonable prejudice?). At that moment, whatever she thought seemed irrelevant. The truth was that I was drawn to this young man who seemed to me almost too good to be true: handsome, intelligent, religious, hard working . . . I laughed to myself as I thought of the litany of virtues in the Girl

3

Scout manual. Maybe I was idealizing him. If so, maybe that was a sign that I was in love. And if that were true, it would be the first time in a very long time.

"It's all right," he told me, "she's just afraid that I'll whisk you off."

"Is that what you're going to do?"

He turned and stared at me for a moment before turning back to watch the road. "Time will tell." Then, after a moment, he added: "Maybe you'll be whisking me off."

I smiled at that. "Yes," I said. "Maybe I will. You'd better watch out."

Tony took me to the movie theater downtown, once known as the Rialto, but now rechristened the Clarksburg Cinema. The old movie house was in a state of slight decay, but back then it still displayed its grand and gaudy rococo style and conveyed an air of defiant opulence. The Cinema maintained an early twentieth-century opera-house charm and had retained its balcony where we sat and necked (while we watched *Ordinary People* with Donald Sutherland and Mary Tyler Moore). Afterward, we drove east on the Boulevard to Hiram's, the popular hamburger and hotdog hangout for the high school and college crowd, where we continued smooching until it was time for him to take me home.

Betty

I wasn't waiting up in the living room with the porch light on when she came home, but I was awake and noted with some satisfaction and maternal pride the respectable time my daughter came in. Perhaps Laura would maintain control of the relationship after all. I sighed in relief and turned onto my side and allowed myself to fall asleep. I worry so much about Laura, about her falling in love with the wrong boy and ruining her life. But, truthfully, I know I probably don't have anything to worry about. She's a sensible girl and practical, like me. I know she'll choose wisely and won't be misled just because some hot guy gets her blood stirred up.

Tony

After taking Laura home that night, after our first date, I drove back to my house on East Fourth Street where I lived with my dad. Alberto Cappeletti, Pop, essentially built our modest home all by himself after he and my mom got married in 1966. My mother died twenty-two years later from cancer. That was only two years ago, in 1988 when I was twenty years old and still a sophomore in college.

When I arrived home, I pulled the car into the driveway. Pop's pickup truck was parked in front of me, meaning that he was home. I knew he was already asleep because the house was dark, so I was extra quiet when I went inside. He works hard and sleeps lightly, so I didn't want to disturb him. After a quick snack in the kitchen, I went up to my room. I had to get up early to go to work at St. Ignatius's Hospital where I was an orderly on weekends and two nights a week when it wasn't during baseball season. From March through May and into June, I played second base on our college baseball team. But, that night I wasn't able to fall asleep right away. I kept thinking of Laura: how pretty she was, how aroused she made me while we were necking in the parking lot out at Hiram's. I was thinking to myself, maybe this is what it feels like to fall in love; I mean to really fall in love.

Laura

I took my time getting undressed and ready for bed. I still felt sexually aroused. I knew that I was going to have sex with Tony and I was looking forward to it. I knew that at some point Tony and I would drive up onto Fairfax Mountain and find a secluded place in the woods where we would make love. Tonight been our first date and I was determined not to appear too easy. Tony was such a good kisser and knew what to do to get me in the mood. I knew how aroused he'd been and I'd been tempted to satisfy him in some way, but it was too soon and I'd fought my impulses. That was the effect that he had on me from the very beginning. I knew my mother was concerned. Any time I dated a good looking boy, she was afraid I'd get pregnant, but I had way too much sense for that.

Betty

Sunday morning Laura and I followed our ritual of going to early mass at St. Joseph's and then to The Cookery on Market Street to indulge in a Sunday morning breakfast that always seemed deliciously decadent compared to our usual Spartan breakfast of a piece of toast and a cup of tea. Sitting in our booth, exchanging an occasional greeting with friends and acquaintances, we caught up on each other's concerns and preoccupations. As mother-daughter relationships go, ours was especially close, I think, and we exchanged more intimacies than you might expect. "So, tell me about your young man," I said.

"Tony thinks you don't approve of him."

I smiled and dabbed at my mouth with my napkin. "So, he's perceptive as well as good looking."

"Tony is very intelligent, maybe smarter than I am."

"Don't sell yourself short, honey. You've yet to meet a male who's as quick as you are."

"Maybe. That might have been true up till now. But Tony really is very bright, Mom. Did I tell you he's pre-med."

"Hmm," I said, sipping at my coffee and turning to look out the window at the passers-by. "I don't recall ever seeing him at church."

Laura laughed. "You're pretty quick yourself, Mom; changing the subject like that."

I paused in the midst of lighting a cigarette. "Where do you think you got it from?"

"I know. Anyway, Tony goes to work early on Sunday mornings. He's an orderly at St. Ignatius on the weekends. That's where we met. He figures it'll help with his goal of becoming a doctor."

"So, in addition to not being Irish, he doesn't go to church."

"Mother! Tony used to be an alter boy. He's probably more religious than I am. He's even active in the Newman Club on campus. And he does go to mass, just not on the weekends when he's working. He usually goes during the week."

"Okay," I said, leaning back, inhaling on my cigarette and then exhaling elegantly the way I'd seen Lauren Bacall do it in the movies. "But, he's still Italian," I reminded her, "and he's still conceited."

"He's not."

"You'll see, honey. Just wait. Those good looking Latins, they only think of themselves. They think they're God's gift and they're entitled to do whatever they want."

"You don't know him, Mom. That's some stereotype left over from a hundred years ago. That's not who Tony is."

I cocked my head and smiled. "Time will tell. Who knows, perhaps you're right after all."

"Just give him a chance, Mom, okay? Don't be a bitch to him."

"Moi?"

Laura laughed. "Just relax, Mom. After all, I'm still a freshman. This was our first date. It's not like we're getting married."

"Married? You're thinking that already?"

"Well, he is special. Who knows? I know it's early and he'll be going to medical school after he graduates next May and I'll still have three more years, and after that . . . ? Maybe grad school. So, no, I'm not planning a wedding. But . . ." she shrugged and smiled, "like I said, he's very special."

"Yeah . . . that's how I felt about your father. I knew right away that he was the one. Just take it slow, kiddo, all right? Like you said, each of you has other priorities."

"I know. Relax. It's cool, Mom."

"Cool. Yeah. Just keep it that way and make your mother happy."

Tony

That was in October of 1990 and I remember that the weather had already started to change. Each day the sun slipped a little lower in the sky and the temperature in our river valley gradually became more brisk and chilly, especially in the evenings. The cooling breeze from the river, so refreshing during the summer, was now a damp chill that, in the winter, when the wind hurtled up the valley from the west, could cut to the bone. Up on Fairfax Mountain, it would get much colder and in winter, heavy snows would make the steep and curvy mountain roads treacherous. Laura and I drove up to the lookout on Fairfax Mountain more than once that autumn, before the cold rains and early snowfalls interfered. We necked and made out in the car and finally—Laura wondered what had taken me so long to get to it—I came equipped with blankets and we laid out on the hard ground in the dark shadows under the trees and made love. She was surprised when I told her that it was my first time and she never could decide, for the rest of her life, if she believed me or not.

That was such a wonderful time, my senior year of college; I'd had girlfriends before Laura, but I'd never experienced anything like what I felt with her. And it wasn't only Laura that made that year so magical. Everything flowed along so smoothly and successfully, it was as if I could do no wrong. Everything worked out for me. I got straight A's in my course work, including my chemistry and zoology courses; was elected co-captain of our baseball team, the Clarksburg Cougars, and hit .317—my highest season batting average ever—and we came damned close to winning our division championship. I may not have been the best second baseman in the league, but I was pretty damned good.

Pop finally let himself get involved in a relationship for the first time since mom died. It made me feel good to see him so energized. He laughed more than he had in a very long time and began to enjoy life again instead of facing each day as if it were a burden he had to stoically bear.

The only thing that marred that year was the fact that by the time graduation rolled around in May of 1991, I had not yet been accepted to medical school. I have to admit, it took me completely by surprise. I had assumed that I'd be accepted somewhere, probably by more than one school, and that I'd be able to have a choice. I'd even allowed myself to expect some kind of scholarship or grant or working assistantship, something that would help with the tuition and other expenses. But, nothing came through. Laura was disappointed for me, but I was stunned. I had worked so hard and done everything right; achieved at the highest level (I graduated summa cum laude) and still I wasn't good enough to be accepted by any of the dozen schools I'd applied to. No acceptance and no financial aid. Pop was crushed. He'd been looking forward to the opportunity of bragging about how his son was going to be a doctor. Now he had to bite his lip and keep his mouth shut.

But, I made up my mind that I wasn't going to quit on my life's dream. I was still determined to become a physician, come hell or high water. I started researching the foreign medical schools in Mexico, the Caribbean, and Italy. In the meantime, I needed a job, a good-paying one that would help finance my goal. Through the help of our long-time family physician, Dr. Gaudino, I was able to get a job as a detail man for one of the pharmaceutical companies.

It was hard work and required a lot of traveling, but I got to know many of the physicians in the area and I developed a close relationship with a number of them. Most were sympathetic to my situation and promised to help if they could. By the fall of '91, I had applied to three schools in Italy, two in Mexico, and one in the Caribbean. Just after Thanksgiving, I heard that I'd been accepted to the medical school in Guadalajara, Mexico. Again, I was shocked that I hadn't received any other acceptances. I had been hoping for one in Italy, maybe Bologna or Milan. But, I was rejected by all of them, as well as the one in Granada in the Caribbean. Guadalajara was the only place where I was accepted and even that was conditional on passing a required Spanish course prior to the opening of the school year. I found out the hard way that I wasn't the hot shit I thought I was.

Laura

I was in the first semester of my sophomore year. Mom invited Tony and his father for Thanksgiving dinner. Alberto asked if he could bring Shirley Thorpe, the widow that he'd been seeing for almost a year. Shirley brought a bouquet of fresh flowers and Al brought two bottles of wine. Mom was a gracious hostess and if she still had any misgivings about Tony, they were not on display. The five of us got along very well. Both Mom and I liked Shirley very much and Al turned out to be less of a peasant than my mother had feared. He was soft-spoken, had no Italian accent (having been born and raised in Clarksburg), was well informed and obviously intelligent—even if not college educated—and had an excellent sense of humor. I was proud of my boyfriend and his father and my mother could see why.

The day after Thanksgiving, Tony called me to tell me that he'd received an acceptance letter from the medical school in Guadalajara, Mexico. I was happy for him and proud too, but I also experienced a sudden sense of fright and dread. Mexico? How would we see each other? What was going to happen to us? How could I survive having him thousands of miles away and not seeing him? Some fellow student, a dark-eyed Mexicali Rose, would steal him away. After all, what would Tony and I have in common once he was immersed in his medical education?

"Classes don't start until the third week of January," he told me, "but I have to take a medical Spanish course and that starts the day after New Years. I'll have to leave here right after Christmas so I can find a place to stay and settle in before classes start."

I felt the tears well up in my eyes. I was going to miss him so much. But, I heard the excitement and the relief in his voice and didn't want to be a killjoy. "I'm so thrilled for you," I told him. But then a sob erupted in my throat and I couldn't hold it back.

"Laura, what's the matter?"

"Nothing. Nothing, really. It's just that I'm going to miss you so much. When will I get to see you?"

"I'm not sure. I've got to go over the finances. I'm not sure when the school breaks are and what the air fare will be. I've got to check it all out."

"Of course. Are you coming over later?"

"Sure. I'll be there (We'd planned to go for a bike ride along the river). I just couldn't wait to tell you the good news. I'll see you in a little while."

Tony

Good news! Well, yeah, I'd been accepted. Finally. But, the truth was, I felt completely overwhelmed by the finances. The tuition alone was over $10,000.00 a year and other fees and living expenses would come to an additional $15,000.00. Twenty-five thousand dollars per year (That was back then. It's almost three times as much now) and it was a six-year program counting the internship—although the last two years were less expensive. Still, all told it would add up to about $150,000.00. The enormity of it finally hit me. A hundred fifty thousand dollars (the equivalent of almost a half million dollars now)! Where the hell was I going to get that kind of money? I would have to pay the first semester's tuition and fees before I could start school: about $8,000.00. And then there would be living expenses, another couple of thousand at least. I had about five thousand saved and I knew my father had been saving some, maybe another ten thousand; the rest I'd have to borrow. With my father's help I could probably cover the first year; but after that . . . ? It was difficult sharing these worries with Laura. I was afraid that I'd come across as defeatist. In truth, part of me wanted to wimp out, stay in my job. I toyed with the idea of working a few more years and saving a lot more. Laura and I would be able to stay together. We might even get married. Maybe I'd stay in pharmaceutical sales. Maybe I didn't have to be a physician. All sorts of things went through my mind. But, I'd underestimated Laura. I didn't appreciate then how loyal, how supportive she could be. Laura had a toughness about her that she got from her mother. It was a real source of strength—for both of us.

When I arrived at Laura's on that Thanksgiving Friday, she'd persuaded her mother to open a bottle of wine so we could all have a drink to celebrate. Betty then left us alone and we sat on the back porch to talk about our future. I explained some of my financial concerns. "Look," she told me, "you're putting the cart before the horse. Get the first year under your belt and see how it goes. If you do well—and I know you will—then, even if they don't give you a grant or a scholarship or an assistantship, you'll be in a better position to borrow the money. You'll have proven that you can do it and no one will have any doubts."

"Yeah, but if I put it off for a year, then I . . ."

"Bullshit, Tony. You're not putting it off. As much as I'll miss you, you can't do that. You've been dreaming of this forever. Who knows, maybe after a successful first year, you'll be able to transfer to a school here in the states. You don't know what will be possible, what might happen."

"Yeah, but us . . ."

"Tony! I know. I'm worried too. I have pictures in my head of some of the female students there—dark-eyed and beautiful and smarter than me—not being able to resist you. And you, being lonely and not being able to say no. You think I don't worry about us?"

"That's not going to happen, Laura. No way."

"Maybe not. I'm just saying that yeah, it'll be tough on us, but if we're meant to be together, we'll get through it. Your only job is to be focused and do your best and then let the chips fall where they may. You can only control what you do. You can't control what'll happen."

"You're right," I said, hugging her.

"You're just too conscientious," she said. "You're trying to control everything and solve all the problems even before they happen. Just take it one step, one semester at a time. We'll work it out. It'll be okay."

"You're right. I've always been like that, building mole hills into mountains, anticipating the worst. But, you're right. We can do this. We will."

We spent the rest of the afternoon riding along the bike path that followed the river. The weather was cool and crisp. The leaves had changed weeks ago and were mostly brown now and littering the path and the ground, leaving the trees nearly bare against a cloudless blue sky. It was a beautiful late autumn day and we glided along full of energy and confidence, enthusiastic about our future. Everything was right. Nothing could go wrong. That night we made love (my father was spending the night at Shirley's) with a renewed urgency as if to store up memories and satisfactions before I would have to leave. And that passion only convinced us more completely of how strong our love was and of our confidence in ourselves and our future together.

In the same spirit, the Christmas holiday assumed more importance than usual. I would be leaving in a few days. The first opportunity for me to visit home would be in June when I had a month off between semesters. But, who knew what would happen? If I'd be able to afford a flight back or if I'd have to do any additional school work to make up for something I'd failed? There was no assurance that I would be able to return home even then.

On December 27th, I left for Guadalajara. It was the first time that I'd been that far from home and the first time I'd flown. Although I had a high school knowledge of Spanish, initially I was overwhelmed when, upon landing, I found myself immersed in everything Spanish—or Mexican. Everything was extraordinarily different: the warm dry weather, the signs on store fronts and streets, the physical look of the people and their manner of dress, the sounds (chatter, background music); and such an expanse of sun and sky. Everything felt warm and open—and dauntingly strange.

The first item on my agenda was to go to the university and to the office of the Registrar and find out about housing. My materials informed me that the Registrar's office would be able to advise me regarding housing. After some miscommunication, I was given a list of addresses. Worn out by the flight and the stress of having to communicate in pigeon-Spanish and pigeon-English, I took the first room I was shown and promptly plopped down on the bare mattress and fell asleep. After napping for a couple of hours, I unpacked and changed and then went out to get a feel for the surrounding neighborhood. I was pleasantly surprised how quickly my high school Spanish came back to me as I recognized what the signs on the store fronts meant and interpreted the headlines in the newspapers. I bought one and vowed to immediately immerse myself in the language.

The next day I completed my registration for the mandatory medical Spanish course and for the beginning of the first semester in medical school. I met some of my fellow students, some of whom were also renting rooms in my building. It was a busy first day, but already I felt more comfortable. I was pleased with the way my Spanish was coming back to me. I was paying more attention to pronunciation, grammar, and the vocabulary than I had in school. Although, for the first two years, classes would be taught mostly in English, after that everything would be in Spanish and I knew that it was to my advantage to become as fluent as possible as quickly as possible. hopefully, my background in Italian, Latin, and college French would also prove to be helpful.

Although I was kept busy with my medical Spanish course, which was very intensive (six hours a day for three weeks), increasingly I felt that I was in my element, that this is where I belonged. I couldn't wait until my medical classes started: anatomy, cellular and molecular biology, biochemistry, histology; and in the second semester: physiology, immunology, embryology and genetics, behavioral sciences, medical ethics, public health and preventive medicine. I felt excited and confident; ready to conquer the world

Every day, I wrote to Laura. I missed her more than I would have thought possible. I felt heart sick and near to despondency when I allowed myself to focus on thoughts of her. I looked forward to her letters but, due to the unpredictability of the Mexican Postal Service, her letters were often delayed for days at a time, even though she too wrote daily. When more than a day went by without receiving a letter from her, I wondered if she had stopped loving me and had found someone else. But, when classes started at the end of January, school work demanded all of my attention and I found myself totally focused. Even though the classes were to be held in English, I tried as often as I could to work with the material in Spanish. I wanted to be as fluent as a native in this language which, with its similarity to Italian, was relatively easily for me.

One of the most pleasant surprises was the weather. Here it was, the end of January, and the daytime temperature was almost always a perfect seventy degrees (F), low humidity, clear blue skies and warm sun. It felt like paradise. I teased Laura, who was struggling with the usual bitter cold and wet winter snows of Pennsylvania as she slogged through the second semester of her sophomore year.

As I settled into the rhythm of going to class, studying, and going through my daily routine, I realized that when the semester ended in the second week of June, I would have two to three weeks when I'd be able to fly back to Clarksburg and see Laura. I looked into air fares and found a flight that would take me home in thirteen hours with a layover in Atlanta and cost $280.00 for a round trip ticket. It was a lot of money, but I figured that I could scrimp on daily expenses and make it. I couldn't wait to write Laura and tell her the good news. Only another four months and we'd be together again.

Laura was thrilled, of course, and made plans to keep those last two weeks of June and the first week of July open so that nothing would interfere with our spending as much time together as possible. She knew how financially strained I was and she made an extra effort to save money that she earned from her job so that she could pick up most of our expenses while I was home. She was so excited she could hardly sleep.

During that first semester of medical school, I did very well. I impressed my teachers with my intelligence and motivation and my classmates with my willingness to help them with their

English. About half of my classmates were Mexican and most of the rest were from Argentina, Chile, Brazil, and other South American countries. Of course, part of my motivation was that by helping them with their English I was also improving my Spanish. Plus, I genuinely liked my classmates and was happy to be able to help them. I developed an especially close friendship with Aristeo Ruiz Acosta, who was from Mexico City. Ari lived a few blocks away in an apartment that he shared with two other students. Ari's father was an executive with a large bank, so Ari had more spending money than most of us. Some of my classmates were even poorer than I was, but I was surprised to discover that there were a number of students whose families were very well off and the expense of medical school was no burden at all. At any rate, Aristeo sometimes insisted on treating me to dinner or drinks in return for my tutoring him in English and I was appreciative. Otherwise, my social life would have been very meager indeed.

When the first semester ended and final exams were over, I was pleased and relieved to find out how well I'd done. I flew home to see my father and Laura full of confidence and certainty that all would go well. Aside from a couple of days when I helped my father with some minor construction projects around the house, and one or two nights when I went out with some of my friends and former teammates, I spent almost every minute with Laura. Our hunger for each other was almost insatiable. Laura told me every little detail of her life over the past six months: her course work, gossip about her friends and classmates, details about her mother's job. I, in turn, told her of all my minor triumphs and frustrations, described my friends and teachers, the room where I lived and the plaza where Aristeo and I hung out when we weren't in the medical school buildings or studying.

When Laura and I made love, we used either a diaphragm that Laura had obtained through Planned Parenthood, or condoms—sometimes both. We were very careful to take precautions to guard against an unwanted pregnancy as neither of us believed in abortion and we both agreed that we would wait until our schooling was over before getting married. The three weeks flew by like three hours and before we realized it, Laura, her mother, Pop and Shirley were seeing me off at the airport; back to Guadalajara and to my second semester.

Leaving Laura, walking away from her after that last kiss, brought tears to my eyes and I began thinking ahead to my next visit home. My final exams would be over during the second week in December and I'd have four weeks before the next semester started. At this point, I no longer had any anxieties about having to stay around school to make up any work. I knew I'd do well.

Once again, I settled into my routine of classes and studying. Most of the time I studied in my room or in the school libraries (In addition to the main library, each department had a smaller and more specialized library). However, sometimes I did my reading at a table in the plaza near my rooming house. Along one side of the plaza was the entrance to a small church. Along another side was a string of small shops that sold drinks, snacks, ice-cream, newspapers, and other odds and ends. Sometimes vendors strolled through selling their wares: clothing, pens, food. I found the plaza charming and relaxing. I could always get a beer or a soda or a burrito and sit at one of the tables under an umbrella and leisurely do my work. Frequently Aristeo was there with me and we'd talk about school or our classmates and teachers, or Ari's girlfriends. He was often in transition between attachments. It was rare for Ari to stay with one girl for more than three or four weeks, and he often teased me about being an old stick-in-the-mud married man.

Near the end of August, Laura wrote that she was late with her period. However, she was often irregular and we had taken precautions (We had joked with each other that we'd done everything to prevent conception except to wear raincoats and galoshes). But, by the end of September, Laura had still not had a period and was beginning to worry. "I don't know if I'm imagining it or not, but I think my boobs are getting bigger," she wrote in one of her letters. Two weeks later she wrote: "I took a home pregnancy test and it showed positive. I went to the doctor at Planned Parenthood and she confirmed that I'm about ten weeks pregnant. I literally think that only God knows how it could have happened. What else could we have done? I'm terribly upset and for some reason think it's my fault. I wonder if I didn't use enough spermicidal jelly or maybe I didn't leave the diaphragm in long enough or insert it correctly. Oh, Tony, what are we going to do? I don't want to get an abortion and don't believe you do either. But having a baby is really going to mess things up for your schooling and mine. And the added expense! How are we going to manage? My mother will have a fit when she finds out and I'll have to tell her very soon. I don't want to have to hide this from her."

I'll admit that my first reaction was anger. I threw the letter across the room as if I could get rid of the unwanted news that easily. I yelled so that my brain couldn't hear Laura's voice in my head telling me what I didn't want to hear. It wasn't really that I was angry, just that the news was so unwelcome and upsetting. Laura was right; the pregnancy presented some very real problems. And, she was also correct in assuming that I, too, was against her having an abortion. Therefore, I concluded, we'd have to get married. She wouldn't be due until March of 1993. That meant that during my visit home in December, we could get married. That was only three months away. Assuming her pregnancy went well, getting married then made sense. But, giving birth in March meant that Laura would have to miss some school; though, if she had to take a couple of incompletes and make it up during the summer, that was doable. But what about raising the baby? Was she supposed to do that all on her own? What was my responsibility? Could she come down to Guadalajara for a semester? For a year? Could we afford it? I wrote to Laura and raised these questions that kept spinning around in my brain and driving me crazy. What did she think?

Between us, we agreed that we'd get married during my visit home in December and that Laura would go ahead and make the arrangements for the wedding. She told her mother and I wrote to my father, telling him all the details. Pop and Shirley met with Betty and decided that they would help the (damned stupid) kids in every way they could. Betty could take off some time from work to help Laura with the baby. This would allow Laura to finish her junior year. Then, in June, maybe Laura and the baby could come to Guadalajara and live with me for the academic year so that at least during the baby's first year, we'd be an intact family. Laura could take the year off from school and the money saved would help pay for her airfare and room and board in Mexico.

Laura and I agreed and I began to keep an eye out for a place that we could afford. Aristeo shook his head in disbelief at his crazy gringo friend. To be in Mexico, surrounded by so many beautiful dark-eyed senoritas, and to be tied down with a wife and baby; what a catastrophe! But, he promised to help me in any way he could. In return, I promised my friend some genuine home-cooked American meals.

Laura

When Tony came home for the holidays, after completing his first year of medical school, I was six months pregnant with our daughter, Jennifer. I couldn't wait to see him. Despite all the loving and reassuring things that Tony said in his frequent letters, I had to see for myself whether or not he was truly happy about our getting married and becoming a father. I felt that I had somehow manipulated him into getting married, that I was at fault, and that he was, underneath his loving words, angry and resentful that I had forced him into this position. But, when I saw him and felt his arms around me and saw the way he smiled at me and my belly, I was reassured. The truth is that he was delighted at the prospect of our being a family. His only concern was our finances and, although he worried about that, he maintained his usual optimistic attitude that somehow things would work out.

We had a small family wedding. It was held in the rectory of St. Joseph's and only our immediate families were there along with my best friend, Susie, and Tony's best friend, Mike. Afterward, we all went out for a special brunch. Tony allowed himself to get a little high on mimosas, but, because of the baby, I didn't have anything to drink other than a sip of champagne. My mom put on a brave face, but I knew that she was disappointed that I'd gotten pregnant and "had" to get married, even though she knew that Tony and I would have gotten married eventually anyway.

To tell the truth, I was a little disappointed too. I'd always dreamt of a big church wedding and a catered celebration in one of the fancy restaurants up on the Boulevard. It's not that I was ashamed of being pregnant. I wasn't. But, I was disappointed that we couldn't have a church wedding and a big reception. But, because of my pregnancy as well as Tony's school expenses, we had to watch every penny we spent.

Aristeo

When Tony returned to Guadalajara after our Christmas break, he was a married man and his friends and classmates teased him mercilessly about it. I found an apartment for Laura and Tony and the baby. Tony settled into it and slowly made it ready for them when they would join him in June during our next semester break. The new apartment was small—only two and a half rooms—and was on the second floor above a taqueria. The little restaurant was open from ten in the morning until one or two in the morning, seven days a week. We Mexicans, we are not afraid to work.

The apartment was convenient to one of the zocolos in the city and Tony imagined Laura bringing the baby there on a daily basis. It was also convenient for shopping and was near the medical school. However, it was noisy. They had to keep the windows open at night because of the heat, but then the noise and smells from down below would permeate their rooms, often keeping them awake.

The rent was more than Tony had been paying for his single room, but it was cheap by today's standards. Laura was busy with Jenny during the day while Tony was at school or studying, but he helped out a little in the morning before he left and in the evening before Jenny went to sleep for the night. Because the crib was in their bedroom and the baby was a light sleeper, Laura and Tony didn't get to make love as often as he thought they would. Besides, for the first several months, Laura was incredibly tired at night.

Looking back, I think it might have been partly post-partum depression and partly hormonal. At the time, neither Tony nor I understood it. How could a young healthy woman be that tired every night? He felt rejected and frustrated and they began to argue about her never being in the mood. The hornier Tony got, the more attractive other women began to look to him. He used to talk to me about it all the time. Every female he saw became a potential sex partner: our female classmates, waitresses at the plaza, women on the street. He must have had fantasies of having sex with dozens, if not hundreds, of women. But, between lack of time, lack of money, and his moral and religious scruples—as well as fear of Laura finding out—he never acted on any of them. Really. I would have known. Still, it was an indicator of the stress on their marriage during that first year.

Tony

I told Ari that I never acted on any of my fantasies. I suppose that technically that is true. Once I started seeing Laura, I was never with anyone else. I never went out with anyone on what you might call a date. But, I was especially attracted to one of the students at school and Alma and I did flirt with each other. Actually, I suggested that we go out and I told her how much I wanted to make love to her. For what it's worth, either she had more moral backbone and self-discipline than I did, or she wasn't interested in me. Who knows? You can never really climb into somebody else's head. Still, I prefer to think that she was attracted to me and did want to get together, but could not overcome her religious upbringing. I guess that was a good thing.

Laura and her mother missed each other. Too much, I thought. Betty sent us care packages weekly, filled with food that we couldn't buy in Mexico. And soap, toothpaste, baby powder, baby oil, and anything else she could think of that we might need or want. Occasionally she'd also slip in a twenty dollar bill or a check. I have to admit, that even though I felt angry about it, later I realized that I felt guilty about having to be dependent on her and upset that I wasn't in a position to be the sole support of my own wife and child. Despite my annoyance at the time, I still realized that Betty was being helpful and I was able appreciate her thoughtfulness. Both Laura and I took a great deal of delight in Jenny. Watching her grow day by day, achieving one developmental milestone after another, was wondrous and miraculous. Our mutual joy in Jenny helped carry Laura and me over the rough spots of that first year.

Laura and Jenny stayed until August of 1994, and by then Jenny was almost a year and a half old and was walking and beginning to talk. Every day I'd come home from school and she would have another word to dazzle me with. Laura had recovered from her fatigue or depression and that summer was a wonderful time, absolutely magical. We were young, happy, in love, and enjoying every minute of our lives. When it came time for Laura and Jenny to leave, to return to Clarksburg, it was a tearful parting for all of us.

Aristeo

It was obvious to me that for the first six months or so, Laura felt the strains of motherhood and adjusting to living with Tony, who was consumed by his classes and studies, and the difficulty of living in a foreign country with a foreign language. By the time Tony finished studying for the day, both of them were exhausted and ready for sleep. Jennifer, who was five months old when they arrived in Guadalajara, was a sensitive baby who woke at the slightest out-of-the-ordinary sound. Somehow, she was oblivious to the loud talking and music that blared from the taqueria downstairs, but the creaking of their bed during lovemaking would make her erupt into loud wailing that could not be ignored. Tony was frustrated by it, but often made a joke of it, saying that he was sure Jenny was doing her best to prevent any siblings from encroaching on her turf. During those months, Laura and Tony argued frequently and I'm sure that their irritability affected Jennifer and made her more difficult. Fortunately, things started to change during the semester break for the Christmas holidays and for the following eight or nine months, until Laura returned to Clarksburg to finish her senior year, it was clear to all of us that they were having a wonderful time together. More than that. They were blissful, and in a way, even I envied their happiness.

During the day, while Tony was at school, Laura made it a point of taking Jennifer to the various plazas, parks, and zocolos around the city, getting to know Guadalajara and its characteristic Mexican charm; meanwhile making a determined effort to learn the language. She and Tony spent a lot of time with his friends from school, especially with me and a female friend of ours, Alma Garcia del Sol. I must tell you that I led Laura into thinking that Alma was my girlfriend. This just made things easier, you understand, because, you know, Tony and Alma had a kind of a thing for each other. Actually, later on, Alma and I did become involved, but back then, we were only good friends. Laura liked Alma and the two of them became quite close. Laura would be upset if I showed up at one of their parties with another young woman for company instead of Alma. I teased Laura about this and told her that I was too young, handsome, and rich to tie myself down to just one pretty seniorita.

When the end of August arrived, Laura cried because she had to return home and leave Tony, her new friends, and the warm enchantment of Mexico. But the cost of her and Jenny staying, and her desire to complete her senior year made it necessary for her to leave. Her tears were contagious, though, and almost all of us cried a little bit when she and Tony parted at the airport. Jenny screamed, saying that she wanted to stay with her daddy. Even Alma and I were affected.

The following month, Tony later told me, Laura was surprised to discover that she was late with her period. She waited a month and when she missed again, she took a home pregnancy test. Once again, despite their attempts at contraception, she had become pregnant. A visit to the doctor confirmed that she would be due in May of 1995. "This is a hell of a way to celebrate graduation," she wrote. Her mother, Betty, was ambivalent: thrilled at the prospect of another grandchild, and surprised that, under the circumstances, her daughter would be so reckless as to allow herself to become pregnant again. "Mom, you wouldn't believe how careful Tony and I were. I can't believe it. I don't know what else I could have done." Although she was upset at what she believed was her daughter's lack of responsibility, Betty accepted Laura's protests and resigned herself to being an active grandmother while her daughter finished her senior year. During this time Betty and Jenny developed a closeness that lasted the rest of their lives.

Tony was shocked to hear the news from Laura. Another child! He was just finishing his second year. He'd still have another three and a half years of schooling after the baby was born. All he could talk to me about was his financial responsibilities and again he wondered if he should quit school and go back to work as a salesman for a pharmaceutical firm. He delayed bringing it up in his letters to Laura, knowing what her reaction would be. And he wondered if it would be better to forego his visit home for the holiday break at the end of the semester and send the airfare money to Laura to help with the expenses for the baby. I convinced him to share his doubts with his father and Al wrote back: "Tony, it's important to all of us, but especially to Laura and Jennifer, that you be here for Christmas. Don't worry about the goddamned airfare. A few hundred dollars one way or the other isn't going to make that much of a difference. Shirley and I are sending you the money for the plane fare. Just concentrate on your studies, do well, and then get your butt up here for the holidays. It feels like forever since we've seen you."

Tony did go home after completing his second year. As a matter of fact, both he and I were at the top of our class. After this year, all of our classes would be in Spanish. Now we were getting into the meat of the program and the demands on our time and energy would increase significantly. He wasn't sure when he'd be going home again as this was going to be a new and more demanding phase of his education.

Betty

While he was home, Tony visited a number of his physician friends to bring them up-to-date on his progress at school. I don't know how he managed to charm them, but more than one volunteered to give him a no-interest loan to help out with his expenses. Tony was overwhelmed with their generosity and vowed to "pass on" this favor and to be a benefactor himself at some point, helping others to achieve their dreams of becoming a doctor.

Tony flew back to Mexico determined to complete his schooling and return home to become a successful physician. He felt he owed it to so many people, he said. He couldn't disappoint them: Laura, me, his father and Shirley, all the people who had contributed to his "fund." I was always uneasy about all of this borrowing, even though I contributed too. Well, what could I do? My daughter and grandchildren were involved. I couldn't abandon them. But I felt uneasy. Who did he think he was that everybody should give him thousands of dollars so that he could pursue his dream? I thought it was very selfish of him, putting all of us in a bind like that. Granted, he did work hard. I can't take that away from him, but the nerve, to feel entitled to get his way like that. And, of course, I was angry because of what I saw him doing to Laura and Jennifer. All that separation and the stress of not knowing how things would turn out. And who knows what he was up to while he was down there? All those Mexican girls and his being so damned good looking. I didn't trust him, I can tell you that. Well, he's a man, isn't he?

Tony returned to Guadalajara with renewed dedication and determination and finished the next four years, which included a year's internship back in the States, in St. Louis, and another mandatory year's clinical work in the hospital in Guadalajara. When he graduated at the end of 1997, Jennifer was four years old and my grandson, Casey, was already two. Laura never went on to graduate school, although she had graduated in the top ten percent of her undergraduate class. Instead, she remained at home taking care of the children and keeping the house for me, who was the sole source of income for our little family during all that time. Al and Shirley often came over and made whatever contributions they could to help us through this period. I liked Shirley. We got along very well and I think she understood my position.

Al

When I look back on those six years that Tony was in Mexico, I feel a great deal of pride and satisfaction. You have to hand it to him. The kid did it all on his own: graduating summa cum laude from a good college, then graduating from medical school near the top of his class—his friend Aristeo barely beat him out for first place honors—and the way he humbled himself, scrounging every nickel he could from just about everybody he knew. And he almost paid everybody back, too; even me and Shirley and Betty, and all the doctors who chipped in. He worked his butt off. His mother, Rosemarie, would have been proud. She wanted to be a doctor herself, you know. She did very well in high school, especially in science, and she wanted to go into medical research, but her father thought that college wasn't for girls and refused to let her go, and she ended up being a secretary. So, when Tony told her he wanted to take a pre-med course in college, she was thrilled. Then she upped and died before he could even finish his undergraduate studies. She would have admired his determination. He never quit. Whatever obstacles came up, he didn't give up. I'm so proud to have a son like that. A doctor.

I think it was primarily because of Rosemarie that he decided he wanted to be a doctor. Ro always had a lot of medical problems and going to the doctor's was always a big part of our life. Dr. Gaudino was like a god in our house. When he suggested that she go to a specialist, like for the surgeries she needed, we always trusted his opinion. He never steered us wrong. Even when she had the miscarriages, he took care of her; and then when Tony was born. It was because of the miscarriages, two of them, that Tony was so special to her. She doted on him. She would have consumed him if I'd let her. Yes, she would have been extremely proud of what he's accomplished and the man, the doctor, he's become.

Tony

When I came back to Clarksburg and finally reunited with my family, I joined the general practice of our family physician, Dr. Mario Gaudino. I was thrilled to be in a general practice and to be able to benefit from the wise, experienced counsel of the man who had helped to deliver me into this world twenty-nine years before. That first year back I felt like my life was a three-ring circus and that I had to be performing in all three of them simultaneously. I had to learn the ways of Mario's office, join the staff of St. Ignatius Hospital and adjust to the different procedures and regulations that governed my professional behavior there. There were a lot of similarities to the way we did things in Mexico, but every hospital has its own way of doing things.

And I had to adjust to living with Laura again. But this time there was also a young daughter, a new son, and my mother-in-law, whose house we lived in until I could afford to put a down payment on a home of our own. Then there were the finances: the money I owed to the banks for school loans and the money I owed private individuals, like Dr. Gaudino, Betty, my dad and Shirley, who had loaned me money to finance my schooling.

That first year, I immersed myself in my work. Naively, I had thought that when I graduated, that I would be a competent physician and that I would have acquired all the knowledge and information that I would need to be successful. However, in my day-to-day practice, I discovered that I was only at the beginning of a long arc of development. Gaudino was constantly giving me little words of advice, telling me anecdotes that had a professional or ethical lesson embedded in them, and counseling me regarding the intricacies and subtleties of hospital and Clarksburg politics. I learned pretty fast and by the end of that first year I was feeling more confidant and had acquired quite a following for myself in Mario's practice. By the end of that year I had also started to pay back some of the money I owed people while still putting aside the beginning of a down payment for a home of our own.

Most importantly, I was home. I was with Laura and my children. Laura and I fell in love with each other all over again, and our bedroom on the top floor of her mother's old house afforded us the privacy we needed to indulge our need for each other. Although we were both surprised when she became pregnant again in spite of our continued use of contraception (condoms plus a diaphragm), this time we only laughed about it. We were sitting pretty and another child, although unplanned for, was more than welcome. But, given our history, I decided to get a vasectomy rather than risk impregnating Laura again. "I have no need to keep you barefoot and pregnant," I told her. So, when our daughter, Mia, was born in March, 2000, we knew it was our last child. Now my family was complete.

Shortly after Laura gave birth to Mia, I surprised her by telling her that I was in a position to buy a house. I still owed everybody money, of course, but I had saved enough for a down payment. We would have our own home. Laura was ecstatic. Betty was more subdued and had mixed feelings. She was glad that she would no longer be subsidizing her son-in-law, and happy that her daughter would have a home of her own, but I knew that she feared losing her bond with Jennifer and Casey; and worried that she might not have the opportunity to develop a relationship with Mia if we weren't all under the same roof.

Betty

1999 was a difficult year for me emotionally. Tony informed Laura that he had saved enough for a down payment on a house of their own and that entire spring was taken up with house hunting and all the confusion and tension that goes with it. She was excited, of course, as were the children; well, at least Jenny and Casey. Mia was a darling and such a cuddly baby. She loved to nestle in your arm and snuggle while she took her bottle. God, I was going to miss her. Tony wanted to move up onto the mountain into one of the fancy new developments. It seemed so far away. I admit that I was angry with Tony that year. In my heart

I blamed him. Everything had to be his way and whatever it was that he wanted, Laura went along with it. I didn't want to lose Laura or any of the children. I didn't want to be left alone in that big house, too big anyway for just one old lady. Well, not too old then, just fifty-two. I tried to convince Laura to stay closer, maybe even within walking distance. "The kids could walk or take their bikes to Grandma's house. You wouldn't have to chauffer them all the time. It'd be great for them." But, in the end, they bought their dream house out on Ridge Road. It meant that Laura would have to drive herself and the kids to everything and I would have to drive out there to see them. Of course, the bus that takes me into work doesn't go anywhere near where they live. Mountain Ridge Estates! Give me a break.

Tony took on a hefty mortgage, but he convinced himself and Laura that it wouldn't be a problem. He was making good money in his practice with Dr. Gaudino and was slowly paying off everybody that he'd borrowed from: me, his father and Shirley, and God knows how many physician friends of his in addition to the regular school loans that he and Al took out through the bank. His ambition and determination had paid off. I couldn't begrudge him that. He'd reached his goal. He was a successful doctor in his home town and everyone was proud of him. All my friends complimented me on what a fine catch my daughter had made. They made Tony out to have been the most eligible bachelor east of the Mississippi. Well, I was proud too. I was. And happy for Laura that she had a husband she could be proud of, who was a father her children loved and could be proud of. And more than that, she was still in love with him. He was her hero. He was everybody's hero. Her only complaint was that he worked too many hours and empathized too deeply for his patients. Well, if you're going to be a beloved family doctor, I guess that comes with the territory.

A couple of years after Tony and Laura moved to their new home, Dr. Gaudino had a stroke and, although he seemed to recover from it, he decided to retire. Tony and he agreed to a buyout. It was another major financial commitment but he couldn't pass up the opportunity. I worried about them, but Laura shushed me any time I brought up the subject of finances and assured me that they were just fine. And, if things got too tight, Tony could always find someone to buy in as a partner. She said it was something he was keeping in his back pocket if he ever needed it. So I said, fine. If they're not worried about their finances, why should I be? After all, the doctor always knows best. Right?

Jenny

I was six when we moved to our house in Mountain Ridge Estates. That's where I grew up and went to school and where all my friends lived. Those ten years were the happiest of my life. I can honestly say that I was very fortunate and had a very happy childhood and that we were the happiest family I knew. Mom was home all the time and Dad seemed to be around when it counted, even though he worked very hard. He left early in the morning to do his rounds at St. Ignatius Hospital and sometimes on weekends he'd have to go in when he was on call, but it didn't seem to stop us from doing things together as a family. My parents often took us to restaurants. We had picnics in the summer and fall. And when we were little my parents often took us to Bertram's Island to a small amusement park. Dad put in a built-in swimming pool and in the summer we spent most of our time there, eating on our patio and having friends over. I had great pool parties. It was an awesome time.

I had a lot of friends then and they all loved my parents. Some of my friends and their parents used my dad as their family doctor and they all thought the world of him. I never heard an unkind word or anything less than expressions of admiration for him. Each of us kids had our own room and Dad said that when I turned seventeen and had demonstrated that I was a responsible driver, I'd get my own car. I couldn't wait. Mom was happy then, too. She kept herself busy with all sorts of things, including taking courses at the university. She planned to go back to work when Mia was old enough. Mia had just turned ten and probably Mom would have gone to work anyway, even if nothing had happened. But, I just wanted to impress upon you that those ten years up on Ridge Road were as close to idyllic as life can get. We were all happy. Everything was great. I guess the law of gravity applies to everything, though, doesn't it?

Laura

I used to think that life was like the transition from day to night. The change from one to the other is so gradual that you don't notice it while it's happening. Rather it suddenly dawns on you that things are different; like watching your children grow: you don't notice it, but suddenly they've outgrown their jeans or their shoes. But, that's not how life always is. Sometimes things change in a heartbeat. One moment you're alive and the next, you're dead from a heart attack, or you got hit by a runaway bus. Bam! Done. Over. Finished. That's how it was for us.

On Monday, April 12, 2010, Tony came home early from work. He collapsed into an easy chair in the living room; ashen, pale as a ghost. I was in the kitchen and heard him come in. I was surprised to hear him come home so early, but I assumed that he'd come into the kitchen with some kind of news or announcement like: "Hey, kiddo, why don't we take the kids and go out for an early dinner?" But, he didn't come into the kitchen. Finally, still holding the carrot I'd been shredding, I walked into the living room to look for him. There he was, sunk into the chair and staring at the ceiling. "What's up, doc?" I joked.

He closed his eyes and slowly shook his head from side to side, as if to say, "Don't ask."

"You okay?" I asked. Again, he just slowly shook his head. I wondered if one of his patients, maybe someone I knew, had died. Maybe his father or somebody we really cared about. "Somebody die?" I asked.

"No," he said slowly. It came out almost as a whisper. "Nobody died."

I pulled up the hassock and sat down in front of him. "What's the matter? What happened?" He opened his eyes and looked at me. His eyes were brimming with tears. I swear, I've never seen him look so sad, like a little boy whose dog had died. "What is it, hon?"

He looked away. "I don't know how to tell you. I can't believe it, that it really happened. It's . . . so fucking crazy."

I suddenly realized that I was still holding that damned carrot. I put it on an end table and knelt beside Tony's chair. "Hon, tell me what happened." It took him some time. I saw him struggling with how to express himself, what words to use, where to start. I forced myself to keep my mouth shut and wait for him to begin.

"They . . . the police, shut down the office."

"What? Why? What for?"

"Some woman, a patient apparently, made a complaint . . ."

"What kind of complaint? Who?"

"I don't know. They wouldn't tell me. They only said that a complaint had been made—I assumed it was a patient—and that the office was a crime scene and that everyone had to leave, immediately. I was in an examining room with a patient for Christ's sake, when I heard the commotion. Then Sally came in and said I had to come out right away. Bastards. They were already telling the people in the waiting room that they had to leave. Sally and Bridget, too; just told them they had to leave immediately and me too. They had a court order. They told me that I couldn't take anything with me, no records or anything. Then they asked for the keys. They were locking everything up and sealing the office. Christ! I said 'What about my patients? How am I supposed to practice if you lock up the goddamned office?' He just looked at me, some detective, Saunders, I think his name was. He had three cops with him. I called Lenny's law firm, but he was in court. Christ, Laura, what am I going to do? What are my patients supposed to do? The office locked down? A crime scene? A fucking crime scene? I don't get it. And they wouldn't tell me anything. Nada."

"Jesus, Tony, what do you think this is all about? Isn't there someone you can ask?"

"I don't know. That's why I called Lenny. I thought he'd be able to find out. Christ, I need a drink."

"I'll get it. What do you want?"

"I don't know. Anything. Something strong. Scotch, maybe."

I went into the kitchen and prepared a drink for him. I felt weak, like the floor had fallen out from under me, with an awful sinking sensation in my stomach. I felt nauseous. Fear! Pure fear! What's going to happen to us? What's this all about? It must be something serious for them to shut down his office like that without any warning. A complaint? Against Tony? I brought the drink back into the living room. He was standing at the window, looking out.

"Here," I said. "Tony, are you sure that this complaint is against you? Is it possible that it might be against someone on your staff?" My legs felt weak and shaky. I had to sit down.

He turned and looked at me. "I hadn't thought about that. Maybe. But, who? What?"

We spent the next hour or so talking about it, trying to figure out what this could possibly be about; what options we had, whether there was anyone we should call. Finally, Lenny, Tony's lawyer, called and Tony told him what had happened and Lenny said he'd get on it immediately. About six o'clock, Lenny showed up at our front door. I made us each a drink and told the kids to make themselves something for supper while we talked. They were aware that there was something terribly wrong and they knew better than to ask what it was. They stayed out of sight the entire evening. Lenny took the drink that I handed him and leaned forward on the sofa. "I spoke to some people I know in the prosecutor's office," he began. "This looks serious, Tony."

"Lenny, I haven't the faintest fucking idea what this is all about. Just come out with it. What's going on?"

Lenny took a deep breath. "It looks like you're being accused of felony sexual assault."

"What?" Tony said. "Assault? Me? Who? Who would accuse me of such a thing? That's impossible. That's fucking crazy."

Lenny shook his head. "I understand that they have at least two women who have come forward independently to lodge complaints against you."

"No way. No way. There's got to be some mistake. I can't imagine anyone who would do that. Who? Who's saying that?"

"I can't tell you the names of the women. I don't know myself. My contact in the prosecutor's office couldn't . . . or wouldn't give me that information. But, apparently, they're both patients of yours. The prosecutor's office has obtained a court order that allows them to comb through your records to see if there are any other victims."

"Victims? Christ, Lenny . . . going through my records? Can they do that? That's all privileged information. That's confidential. They can't do that, can they?"

Lenny nodded. "Yeah, actually, they can."

"What about the office? When can I open up the office? I've got patients. Appointments."

"I don't know. You could be closed down for a while."

"But, there must be something we can do . . ."

"I'll try to get a restraining order to stop them from combing through your records and closing the office, but, frankly, Tony, I don't think the judge will grant it in this case."

"But, I didn't do anything. Jesus, Lenny, they can't just shut down my whole practice on some crazy . . . accusation. This is insane. It's not right."

"Look, Tony, this is very serious. Two of your female patients have accused you of improper behavior. Criminal behavior. If you were guilty . . ."

"But, I'm not . . ."

"I'm just saying, if you were guilty and the authorities didn't do anything to stop you from assaulting more women . . ."

"Jesus, Lenny, do you hear yourself? Do you fucking hear what you're saying?"

"Calm down. I'm only saying that they're watching their own ass. They've got to cover themselves."

"From what? What is it I'm supposed to have done?"

Lenny shook his head. "Tony, I don't have any specifics. Tomorrow I'll talk to some more people and find out what's going on. But, for now, just sit tight. Tell your staff and your answering service that the office will probably be closed for a few days. You don't have to give any explanation. Oh, and if anybody from the papers or TV calls, don't talk to them, okay? You hear me? You too, Laura, no comment. Don't even talk to them. Hang up. Nothing. Not a word, all right?"

When Lenny mentioned the press and the TV, it was like I'd been shot. Holy shit, I thought, everybody is going to know. Tony will be tried in the media. Oh my God, people actually are going to believe this crap. They'll think where there's smoke, there's fire and they'll believe he's done something terrible. Then I thought about the kids. What will they be hearing? What will other kids be saying at school? Kids can be mean. What's going to happen to us? To all of us? Again, that sick sinking sensation in my stomach, an immense empty void where once the solid center of my being used to be. I flushed with shame and fear; first hot and sweaty, then clammy cold. What could we do to protect ourselves? The room tilted a bit and I felt woozy and held on tightly to the arm of the chair. I looked at Tony. His jaw was set in grim determination, but fear was in his eyes. Reflexively I reached to him and grabbed his hand. I don't know if I was holding on for support or trying to let him know that I was with him. Perhaps both.

After Lenny left, Tony was grim-faced and mumbling something about getting everything straightened out and not to worry. Afterwards, Tony and I collapsed onto the living room sofa. We tried to talk, but could only voice our worst fears. The kids came in and asked what was happening. Tony said that we didn't really know, that apparently someone had made some kind of accusation and the police had closed down the office and Lenny would try to find out what it was all about. It had to be some horrible mistake, but in the meantime, he had sort of an enforced vacation.

The next day it was in the papers and on the local TV: Two unnamed women had accused Tony of sexually molesting them in the office and the County Prosecutor's office had shut down the practice pending further investigation. The phone began to ring and didn't stop: reporters, friends, anonymous enemies; the friends with words of support and the faceless cowards with unspeakable vile epithets. We stopped answering the phone and left it off the hook.

Jenny

When the story first came out in the Clarksburg Crier and on TV, everyone wanted to know if it was true and at first I said it was some stupid mistake and my father was trying to find out who was responsible. But, then it dragged on and as more news came out I felt more and more vulnerable. Most kids were nice and never brought it up. Nobody hassled me about it. Some kids avoided me, I know, but mostly, they avoided the topic. I know I never brought it up myself. Casey said it was pretty much the same for him. But, even so, everyday I lived with the fear that all my friends would abandon me. I had this fantasy that maybe they didn't know, maybe they hadn't heard, maybe their parents hadn't told them. Now I know that that was stupid. Of course they knew. It's only that I didn't want them to know. I felt so ashamed. Ashamed of what my father was being accused of, ashamed of doubting if he really was innocent. What if the accusations were true? My God, my father some sort of pervert? I wanted to believe he was innocent, that everyone else was lying. But . . . what if they weren't? What if he was the one who was lying? I never shared that thought with anyone; not my mother, not even my brother; certainly not my little sister. God!

Tony

The next day the story was in the papers and it remained there almost on a daily basis. Every day brought some new revelation leaked to the press, and each new smidgeon of information became an excuse for the media to revisit the whole sordid story.

There was a leak that the prosecutor's office was looking for other possible victims and was inviting current and former patients to come forward with their suspicions or accusations. Then I found out that the State Board of Medical Examiners had suspended my license. "Jesus Christ, Laura, did you seen this? The fucking Board of Examiners has suspended my license."

"Can they do that? Before you're even brought to trial? No one has even found you guilty of anything."

"They haven't even brought an indictment against me. As of now, there still aren't any charges. Jesus."

I called Lenny and blew off some steam, but there wasn't anything he could do. He said he'd look into it. Maybe he could get a stay or something. Then, of course, the hospital called. Dr. Stavrous, the Chief of Staff, told me that the Board had voted to suspend my hospital privileges. Oh, he was nice about it, sympathetic and suave as ever, but all the same, he slid the scalpel in very smoothly and unerringly found the artery that guaranteed that I'd bleed to death. After I calmed down, I realized that he had no choice. Of course, if my license was suspended, how could he let me continue on their staff? It was impossible. It soon became crystal clear that my office was going to be closed for a very long time; perhaps months, maybe longer. Maybe I'd never get my license back, never be able to practice medicine again. I began to feel like my life was over. What would I do? How was I supposed to earn a living? Support my family? Send my kids to school? Pay off the loans to everyone I owed money to?

My father and Shirley and everyone in the family were supportive and tried to be encouraging, but it was all bullshit. I mean, they had no way of knowing what was going to happen, so how could they be reassuring? They meant well, but their words had no meaning. They didn't know what they were talking about.

Laura

Soon there were stories in the papers and on the local TV and radio, that more women had come forward. There ended up being a total of eight, including the original two, although none of the names had been revealed, so there was no way for Tony to defend himself. But the number eight seemed to be, in itself, overwhelming evidence that he was guilty—although we still didn't know exactly of what. "Inappropriate sexual behavior. Felony sexual assault. What the hell does that mean?" Tony was furious. He nagged Lenny and Bernie Spector, a specialist in defending physicians against charges of malpractice that Lenny brought in, to be allowed to make some statement in his own defense, either to the grand jury or to the police or to the press; but Lenny and Bernie were dead set against it. "Time enough for that later," they said. So here we were, weeks later, with Tony's reputation in shambles, his medical practice ruined, his license suspended and his hospital privileges withdrawn. He's prosecuted daily in the press and found guilty of doing something horrible and yet he's never even been questioned by the police. No one officially has asked him one goddamned question. And me, and the kids, and my mother, and his father and Shirley, we're all paying a price, a heavy fucking price, and there's not a damn thing we can do about it.

Tony, as you might expect, stopped approaching me for sex. He was still attentive and affectionate and caring, but it was as if he'd lost interest in sex. God knows what he was thinking. I asked him a couple of times, but he just shook his head and apologized. He said that as a result of all this, thinking about sex made him feel dirty. I think there were tears in his eyes, but I'm not sure. He turned away. I don't know. Maybe part of it was my fault. Maybe I'd shied away from having sex with him, wondering if he had in fact been doing things with other women. I pictured him doing things with them that he did with me. I didn't believe it. I didn't. But, if I'm honest, I did wonder. Maybe I too had found him guilty of something—something unspeakable, something slimy and unknowable, something I didn't want to know about, or even think about—and I didn't want to have anything to do with him that way. I don't know anymore what I thought or believed or felt. So, yes, the strain affected us. In many different ways.

Tony

Lenny and Bernie, my 'Dynamic Duo,' found out the names of the first two women who had accused me. The first one to make an accusation was Linda Davidson and the second was Toni Fernandez. This was our first big break. Linda was the mistress of the sheriff, Billy Cobb. And (Bernie's investigator discovered) Toni Fernandez was a friend of Linda's and lived in the same apartment complex. Linda had been a patient of mine for some time and I'd always found her pleasant. She had told me herself of her relationship with Sheriff Cobb, and, in fact, I'd tested her for STDs because she'd been concerned that he might have been cheating on her as well as his wife. And Toni Fernandez had only been in my office once, trying to con me into giving her a prescription for pain killers, which of course, I didn't do. I understood her being pissed at me for that, but why accuse me of doing something sexual to her? And Linda? After all this time to accuse me of something like that? Why? Then it occurred to me. Right away I called Lenny and told him I had to see him and Bernie right away. They suggested that I come right over to their office, which was downtown near the courthouse.

"A few months ago," I told them, "a patient of mine, a man named Turley, got arrested on a drunk and disorderly. He'd started a fight in a bar and did some damage to the premises as well as seriously injuring someone. His family couldn't make bail and he ended up in our county jail to await trial. As part of my duties as the physician at the county jail, I examined him. I knew he had a history of diabetes because he had been a patient of mine for some time. You know the sheriff runs the jail? So, after I examined the prisoner I told Cobb about his condition and wrote a report that Mr. Turley needed a special diet and that he should be monitored and that he had to have access to his insulin medication. Cobb barely acknowledged what I said and apparently paid no attention whatsoever to my report. The man died a few days later because those idiots neglected to follow my directions. He went into a diabetic coma and they did nothing. He fucking died because of them. It was pure negligence on their part. He had no access to medication and they never monitored his blood sugar level. They never called me or anyone else to treat him. Joe Turley died because of Cobb's negligence.

"His wife brought a wrongful death suit against the city, the county, and the sheriff and they asked me to be their main witness against Cobb. That's got to be why this is happening. It's all because of that wrongful death suit. It has to be. Cobb is afraid of being kicked out of office, losing his job, his reputation, payoffs, who knows what. And if they found him guilty, he'd be sued, maybe for millions. He couldn't let that happen, don't you see? He had to do something. I was the main witness against him. If I'm eliminated as a threat, he's home free. He must have told his girlfriend to come up with this cockamamie story of sexual assault to discredit me. Then she enlisted her girlfriend, Toni, to make it seem all the more believable."

"But, how do you explain all the other women? Six additional women?" Bernie asked. "Are you saying that Cobb got eight women to perjure themselves?"

"I don't know. I don't even know who they are, so how can I say? God knows what their motivation might be. I only know I never did anything remotely wrong to anybody. I never abused anyone in my whole life. So I know that whatever it is they're saying, it has to be a lie. But, I can't tell you why they're doing it."

"Well," Lenny said, "we won't know who they are or what they're accusing you of until the grand jury issues an indictment and you're actually charged. At that point they'll have to share with us whatever evidence they have."

"Not before then?" Both Lenny and Bernie shook their heads. "But when will that be?" I asked. "How long is this going to take?"

Bernie looked at me. "As long as they want it to take, doctor. It could be a few more weeks. Probably longer."

"Meanwhile, I have to sit on my hands? What am I supposed to do? They've shut down my practice and taken away my license. My kids are going through hell at school. There must be something I can do."

"No. Unfortunately, you just sit tight and get through this as well as you can. But I must tell you, Tony, assuming the grand jury indicts you and you are charged, we'll need to start preparing to go to trial. We'll need you to pay us another installment on our retainer at that time."

"I've already given you fifty thousand. How much more will you need?"

"Doctor, that's when the real work begins and the hours pile up. We'll have the names and statements of their witnesses then, their sworn depositions. There's a lot we'll have to investigate. We'll need at least another hundred and fifty thousand then and possibly more later on, once the actual trial starts."

"Another hundred and fifty thousand? Jesus, Lenny, where am I going to raise that?"

"Your malpractice insurance should cover it," Lenny said. "Have you explored that with them?"

"I did. They told me that it didn't cover if I was charged with a felony. That's what I'll be charged with, right?"

"Unfortunately, yes. I'm sure there will be multiple counts. I'm sorry, Tony, but this will be expensive. You should prepare for a long drawn-out process."

On the way home from their office, I was angry and scared. They hadn't paid any attention at all to my information. It was crystal clear to me that Cobb had engineered this whole farce in order to protect himself. Yet, neither Lenny nor Bernie seemed to give it any importance at all. And another hundred and fifty thousand dollars? And then maybe even more down the road? Where was it all supposed to come from? There was no money coming in and nothing left in savings. I needed money to live on, to pay the mortgage, buy food and pay my debts: the tuition at St. Joseph's for the kids, and the car payments, and medical insurance. This could drag on for months yet even before a trial started. Then they'd probably ask for more money. Jesus. How much more? And I wasn't supposed to say anything? Wasn't supposed to defend myself? Didn't the police or the prosecutor even want to hear my side? Didn't they care about what I had to say? Innocent till proven guilty? Bullshit! I was guilty in everyone's eyes until I could prove that I was innocent and how was I supposed to do that?

Laura

When Tony told me about the money, I was shocked. I had no idea that defending himself would cost that much money. Meanwhile, what were we supposed to do? How were we supposed to live? I was reluctant to share any of this with anyone. I didn't want the kids to worry and, frankly, I was afraid of what my mother might say, or at least think. All she had to do sometimes was raise an eyebrow to make me feel like a complete idiot. She never said anything against Tony, but I knew that she wondered if he might actually be guilty. Hell, I sometimes wondered that myself.

Jenny

During this time my attitudes toward sex changed drastically. Instead of thinking of sex as something mysterious and romantic, something to look forward to, but be careful about, I began to feel that it was a dirty and detestable thing. I wondered what it was, exactly, that my father was supposed to have done. Feel up women's breasts while pretending to give them a breast exam? Have sex with them? I mean, actually doing it? I didn't want to think about it. The idea of my father having sex with all those women; someone had to be lying, either those eight women or my father. Of course I couldn't say anything. He was my father. I loved him, but in spite of myself, I slowly began to mistrust him. I began to look at him differently. I saw him as a man, not just my father. I saw him as someone capable of having sexual feelings and passions, not just my asexual father. It frightened me. It was revolting. Who was he? Who was I? I was his daughter and supposed to be loyal. I was supposed to believe in him. And I did. I did. But, I wondered . . . I worried that I might be wrong. I didn't know what to do. I put on a smiley face and pretended everything was all right, that nothing had changed, but it was a lie. I felt so alone. What was going to happen to us?

Shirley

You might think that because I was the Johnny-come-lately to this family, that I would be the least involved. After all, I wasn't even really a step-mother, given that Tony was all grown when I came on the scene; and then he was away, down in Mexico, for all that time. Still, I didn't feel left out of all this drama that everyone was going through. I went through it too, although not as much as Al did. Reading stories in the newspaper every day about all those women saying Tony did those things to them really tore him up. We stopped going to places where people knew us. If we went out to eat, we went out of town and we didn't use a credit card. People would see the name Cappeletti and you'd see them do a double-take. And even when they didn't say anything, you could see Al wince and tighten up. He always defended Tony. Well, so did I. So did we all, everyone in the family. And nobody ever said anything directly to me that wasn't supportive or sympathetic. But, we all knew what everyone was thinking: how could eight women all be wrong about something like this? Even though no one knew any of the details and nothing had been reported, there were all kinds of rumors and crude remarks being made. I felt sorriest for Al, of course. He was so shaken by this. But, I also felt sorry for Laura and the kids. God, it was awful, just awful. It broke my heart out just to think about them. And underneath it all, hidden away from everyone, I was angry, angry at Tony. What had he done to bring the whole world crashing down on all of us? He must have done something.

Aristeo

After Guadalajara, I did a residency in psychiatry and opened a practice in Mexico City. I was doing very well. You can imagine how completely surprised I was when I heard from Tony out of the blue after so many years. But we had been very close in medical school, so I wasn't surprised that he turned to me as a confidante. But the nature of his difficulty, I was flabbergasted, as you say in English. He told me that, contrary to the usual procedure, the state had taken away his medical license based only on accusations of wrongdoing, even before any legal charges had been brought against him. In addition the police closed his office and he had his hospital privileges revoked. There was absolutely no way for him to earn any income and yet he had enormous bills: mortgage, car payments, loans, school tuitions, etc., not to mention his lawyers. He asked me how was it possible for these women to come forward and accuse him without his having done anything wrong to them. He had no explanation for it. He shared with me his hypothesis about the first two women having accused him of sexual abuse at the instigation of the county sheriff who was responsible for the running of the county jail and who was being sued for negligent homicide for having allowed a prisoner to die for lack of proper medical attention. That he could understand. Those women had a reason for wanting to make Tony look bad. But, what about the other six women?

I told him that there might be many reasons. Once the story was in the papers, for example, if the detectives asked leading questions of his female patients, the women might respond to subtle suggestions and be led to believe that he had done something to them that he should not have done and that they had been taken advantage of in some way. Also, I explained that many women have a history of being sexually abused and once the question is raised, might be all too ready to believe that they had been victimized again. It was hard to tell without knowing details, but I assured him that there were many examples in the literature of the media creating a climate of hysteria resulting in all kinds of bizarre accusations. For example, in one famous case young children swore under oath that their teachers had forced them to engage in naked sexual games with dinosaurs and giraffes as well as with each other and their teachers. I told him that I knew the specifics were totally different, but the point was that it was well established that people are suggestible and can be led into believing all sorts of things that are not true and that it was entirely possible that some of these women were led to believe that they had been victimized even if it weren't true.

Still, I couldn't believe it. Why had this happened to Tony? He was the most straight-arrow guy I'd ever known. Of all people to be accused of sexually abusing his patients, he's the last guy I'd have ever thought of. I wished him well, of course, and reassured him that I believed in him and sent him a check for ten thousand dollars. I told him to think of it as a loan if he wished, but it was really a gift. He wrote back and thanked me for my loyalty and reassurance most of all and promised to pay back the loan when things got back to normal.

Tony

After four months of purgatory, the grand jury finally came out with an indictment and we had the list of women who had made the accusations plus the details of their sworn statements. It made for horrifying reading. Aside from the first two, who had clearly perjured themselves, the rest were all long-time patients of mine. I was shocked that these women could have brought themselves to make these crazy allegations against me. They testified that even though they had come in to my office with some minor complaint like a cold or headache, I had persuaded them to agree to let me do an internal exam, and then, under the pretense of giving them a gynecological exam, I stimulated and fondled their clitoris and vagina; or gave them unnecessary breast exams and made suggestive remarks. I couldn't believe how they'd distorted what had happened. But more than that, I was furious that they could ignore all the good that I had done for them and their families and allow themselves to be pressured into making such ludicrous statements. How could they lie like that? How could they live with themselves? I was furious and as soon as I finished reading the grand jury report, I called Lenny and Bernie. "These are all crazy lies. I can prove it. I know they won't be able to say these things to my face. They can't. It's impossible." They both said that they would have their investigators on it and that they were sure we'd be able to put up a strong defense. Now was when the real work started, they said, and when they needed more money.

Now that I'd been indicted, there would be a number of legal proceedings. I'd have to go to court to plead not guilty and have bail set. There would be another court appearance to set the date of the trial, and so on. During this time, my attorneys called me into their office to share the information that their investigators had uncovered.

Lenny told me that the city of Clarksburg was engaged in a project to build a major office and retail center near the center of town. It was to be the home office of a major bank and would contain a key retail outlet and high rent office space. It would be a major coup for the city and bring in lots of good jobs and significant tax revenues. There was much political infighting going on behind the scenes and most of it had not been made public. The promoters of the project had been quietly buying up property downtown for the center and the city was giving large tax breaks to lure prospective tenants to our city.

There was, of course, some resistance to the city acquiring the necessary properties; long-time owners of these properties didn't necessarily want to sell and have to move their businesses. Some of the residents wanted to keep the small-town flavor of downtown and didn't want to modernize and replace the historic architecture with a new high-rise mega-office and retail center. As sheriff, Cobb had been able to pressure some of the property owners to sell.

I had heard rumors of some of this for some time but hadn't paid much attention. Lenny told me that their investigators had discovered that one of the partnerships involved in promoting this project and which stood to make millions of dollars if the project were realized, had a corporation named Harco Limited as one of its members. A major stockholder and member of the board of trustees of Harco Ltd, was Billy Cobb's wife. "It would seem," Bernie concluded, "that if you were to testify successfully against Sheriff Cobb in that wrongful death suit, there might be some ramifications. It would put him in a bad light and ruin his reputation, maybe get him kicked out of office. And his wife's role in this real estate scheme would be pointed to. It wouldn't look good. His wife's reputation would be tainted by his conviction and the whole deal would smell of corruption. Those opposing this major redevelopment project for downtown would definitely use it against him. There's a lot of money riding on this project, Tony, and if it stalls because you put the sheriff in legal hot water, a lot of people could stand to lose a great deal of money."

"Great," I said. "So we can show that he has a motive to discredit me."

"Well," Lenny drawled, "hopefully we would be able to bring that out and show its relevance. But, of course, he'd deny that his wife's investments had anything to do with the complaints that were brought against you and we'd still have to be able to defend you against the accusations of eight women, only two of whom have any connection to Cobb. That leaves six women who don't appear to have any ulterior motive for bringing charges against you."

I could tell from the looks on their faces that they weren't optimistic. "So, what are you saying, Lenny?"

Lenny and Bernie looked at each other. Bernie spoke. "I expect, doctor, that the prosecutor may bring up the subject of a plea bargain. Depending on what they offer, it may be something that you might want to consider."

"A plea bargain? What would be involved in that?"

"Well, like I said, we don't know yet what they might offer, but it's usual in situations like this for them to offer a lesser charge which would carry with it a lesser penalty in return for a guilty plea. In your case, it would probably be a misdemeanor charge of some sort."

"A guilty plea? But Bernie, I've told you, I didn't do anything. I'm not guilty of anything."

"Tony, your guilt or innocence isn't the issue here. If you are found guilty of the numerous felony charges brought against you,

you could be in prison for the next sixty years if the sentences were to run consecutively. You have to consider what that would mean for you and your family, your wife and children."

"And your father," piped in Bernie.

"What are you saying? That I should plead guilty to something I didn't do? Because if I don't, I'll spend the rest of my life in prison?"

"We're not suggesting anything," Lenny said. "Actually, it would be improper for us to do so. We're only saying that the prosecution will probably come forward with some sort of plea bargain deal and that when that happens, you shouldn't reject it out of hand, even if you are innocent."

"But I am innocent!"

Laura

When the lawyers sent Tony a copy of the grand jury report, Tony took it into his study to read. After an hour or so, I went in. He was sitting at his desk with the report open in front of him and staring into space, shaking his head back and forth in disbelief.

"How bad is it?" I asked him.

He gave a thumbs-down. "Go ahead. Read it. I can't believe these bitches. For all these years, I thought they liked me, respected me, were appreciative of all I did for them and their kids. And now I get this. This shit. Thrown in my face. I don't understand it. I can't."

I picked the report up from his desk and sat down on the love seat by the window and began to read. Most of the women's names were familiar to me. A couple of them were the mothers of Jennifer's friends. Some I'd heard Tony mention. I was shocked at what they'd accused my husband of: masturbating them, groping them. One was even sure that he masturbated himself out of her view while she lay exposed. Every once in a while, I glanced up and looked at him. Could any of this possibly be true? Was my husband capable of this kind of behavior? No, I said. Not the man I know. The Tony I know is too professional, conscientious, too respectful, too inhibited to even think of taking advantage of a woman in such an aggressive, predatory way. That isn't who he is. Could he find another woman attractive? Of course he could, and did. I know. There have been a couple of times during our marriage when I sensed that he had a crush or an attraction to a particular woman and we discussed it and we nipped it in the bud. But this? This adolescent bullshit? This was the stuff of someone else's fantasy. This wasn't him. When I'd read enough, I tossed it down and told him that I didn't believe a word of it.

"This isn't you, Tony. Anybody who knows you will know this isn't true. These women are wrong." Tony nodded and sighed. I assumed that he was relieved that I felt that way. "My only question is why. Why are these women . . . why are they saying such things?"

"I don't know, Laura. I can't really figure it out. I wrote to Aristeo and asked him what he thought. He said that maybe some of them might have had a history of sexual abuse and might have been easily convinced that they had been victimized again. I don't know."

"But, the things they're saying, Tony, that you masturbated them. Are they just making that up from whole cloth? Are they hallucinating?"

"Maybe they are. How the hell should I know? Who knows why some people say or do crazy things?"

"But, you must have done something to them. All these women saying almost the same thing; they all couldn't just be making it up, could they? I mean you had to be doing something to them. What were you doing?"

"Jesus, Laura, what do you think? All I ever did was examine them or treat them. I was their family doctor. I did what any doctor does, what any physician would do."

"But some of them said they came in with a cough and you gave them an internal."

"No, that's not what happened. Look, sometimes, yeah, their initial complaint, what first brought them in, might have been something mild: a cough, a headache, an infection, whatever. And if they were a new patient, I'd take a history, as I always do with a new patient. And I'd ask them if they had a gynecologist and if they said no, I'd ask them if they wanted me to do an internal exam. Otherwise I could refer them to a gynecologist. If they said that they wanted me to do the exam, then I would. That's it. It's as simple as that. I run a general practice, a family practice. I do everything."

"And those women who said you masturbated them, what did you do to them?"

"Jesus, Laura, you sound . . ."

"I'm just saying, Tony, that you must have done something that they might have misinterpreted."

I saw that Tony was getting exasperated and defensive. "I don't know, hon. The only thing I've been able to figure out is that sometimes I'd notice that some women patients didn't practice very good hygiene and when I examined their genital area, sometimes I'd find irritation, inflammation in the folds of their labia. If I did, I'd explain to them why the tissues had become inflamed and I'd clean it and put a little Bacitracin on with a cue tip. Then I'd instruct them on how to keep themselves clean. That's the only thing I've been able to come up with. But how anyone could misinterpret that and say I was masturbating them . . ."

Part of me agreed with him, but I also understood that many women might feel uncomfortable with that. "But, surely they wouldn't think you'd dare to molest them with Sally or Bridget standing there. Couldn't they testify that . . ."

"No."

"No? Why not?"

Tony looked away from me.

"You mean that you didn't have a nurse in the examining room with you?"

"I never thought it was necessary. Christ, Laura, If I had a nurse in the examining room with me for every patient . . . do you realize how much extra that would have cost me? I've got bills, Laura. There are people I owe money to, including your mother and my father; school tuitions, what I owe Mario for buying his practice. I can't afford to hire another full-time nurse just to hold somebody's hand. Besides, I didn't think it was necessary. I know these people. I'm a professional, a damned good doctor. I know what I'm doing. I never did anything that would give anyone reason to accuse me of malpractice. I never thought that something like this could happen, that people could be like this. I just never saw it coming."

Betty

Oh, the newspapers had a field day when the grand jury report came out. It seemed to me that it was the only thing that people talked about. Everyone I met in town seemed to start their conversation with some expression of sympathy for me and what poor Laura and those beautiful children must be going through. Nobody ever called Tony a pervert or a sex maniac to my face, but that was the implication. Poor Laura, married to a pervert. You could hear their minds whirring away: a pervert like that! Are his own children safe? How can Laura continue to live with him? Oh the poor girl. It was beyond shame, beyond embarrassment. What could I say? What could I say to my own daughter? I told you so?

Tony finally realized that they had to sell the house. They had to come up with another hundred and fifty thousand dollars for the lawyers and there was no money coming in. They squeezed into my house, all five of them. You can imagine how I felt, having him there under the same roof with me. I felt like I was harboring a criminal, some escaped convict. I wanted to scream, "Here he is. Come and get him." But, because of Laura and the kids I was powerless. What was I supposed to do? Turn them out on the street? Al and Shirley would have helped—and they did, financially—but they didn't have the room that I did. Although, sometimes they'd take the kids for a weekend, just to give us all a break.

You can imagine the tension with the six of us living on top of each other. Electric. Everyone was irritable. Touchy. You couldn't look at anyone cross-eyed without it causing an argument. I don't know who was worse, but certainly Tony was defensive as all hell, a ticking bomb ready to explode at any moment. And he was at his worst with his kids. Those poor children. They needed so much support, but he was hardest with them. He complained about every little thing, not just their school work. It's as if *they* had to be perfect to make up for his imperfections. Or maybe he just had to demonstrate that he was still the man of the family, that he was still entitled to some respect.

Tony was no longer the young Lothario, the young Roman God, the athletic wonder. He stayed home, in *my* house, hidden from the public except for when he went to his lawyers or to his dad's place. He just sat and ate or drank and stared gloomily out the window or just plain moped around. He got sullen and sloppy. He was sorry for himself and irritable with everyone around him. Well, the taller the tree . . .

I kept out of his way as much as I could. Thank God I was still working. School was my refuge and somebody had to bring in some money. Laura tried hard to get a job. God bless her, she went out every day answering ads, knocking on doors, but jobs weren't so easy to come by. I wondered what would happen to her and the kids if Mr. Wonderful ended up going to prison for God-knows-how-long. Christ, I hoped that didn't happen. Well, at least they'd be able to continue living with me. I felt more grateful than ever for what my husband had provided for us. If only he knew that I'd still have to take care of our daughter and grandchildren after all this time.

Tony

Six months after that fateful day when they shut down my office, Laura and I and our three kids were back living with my mother-in-law. We sold our home to raise cash for the lawyers and, unfortunately, it was in the middle of a recession and a housing slump, so I was barely able to pay off our mortgage and have enough left over for Leonard and Bernie. I was out of work, having lost my license and my hospital privileges. And now,

I'd lost my house too. I still don't understand how the Board of Medical Examiners could do that to me without my ever having been found guilty of anything. My kids were no longer attending St. Joseph's. Even with all that I'd contributed to the school and the fact that their grandmother worked there, they wouldn't waive the tuitions for the kids. I'd sold my Mercedes and Laura sold her SUV and we picked up a second-hand minivan.

Our parents were supporting us again, as they had when we were in college. Laura and I had reached the point of applying for welfare. We were now on Medicaid and receiving a monthly allotment of food stamps. Me, a physician, who had a thriving practice; now my family and I are on food stamps and Medicaid and welfare. Can you fucking believe it? And the Board of Medical Examiners and the prosecutor's office, they don't care. Do you know that I still have never been given the chance to tell my side of the story? Over six months now and no one has ever asked me what happened. You would think that the police, who closed me down and shut my office, or the prosecutor who's using my tax dollars to prosecute me would say, "Hey, Dr. Cappeletti, these women have made these accusations against you. What's the story? What do you have to say about that? But, no. They don't care. And this is America? This kind of shit can happen here? And it's not even a fucking police state like China or Russia. Christ!

Al

Thank God I have Shirley in my life. I don't know what I'd do without her. If Rose had been alive to see this, it would have killed her. But, with Shirley, it's not the same. She's not his mother, you know? It makes a big difference even though she loves him and thinks the world of him. So, she's been able to stay strong through all of this and she's been there for me. I know how lucky I am in that regard. I don't take her for granted, not for one minute. But, Tony . . . he's going through hell. Most of the time he doesn't want to talk about it with me. I ask him how he's doing and he tries to smile and tell me everything is okay and under control, that his lawyers are on top of things and when it finally goes to trial the truth will come out and everything will be all right again. That's what he says, anyway. I'd like to believe him. I want to believe him. But I don't know. From what I hear and see around me, I'm afraid that everybody is already convinced that he's guilty. You wouldn't believe the phone calls I get; two o'clock in the morning, obscenities, threats. You'd think I'd raised a monster, that I was personally responsible or that it's inherent in our Italian blood. What else can you expect from a goddamned guinea? I can only imagine what it's like for Laura and the kids.

Shirley and I have the grandkids over sometimes for the weekend, just to give everybody a break. I see how it's affected them, even little Mia. Shirley and I try to help out. Financially, we do what we can, but this thing has just consumed money like—I don't know what—like an incinerator. It just goes. Poof! Up in smoke. Gone. We might as well be burning it for all the good it's done so far. Maybe when we finally get to the trial, we'll see the results of all this. Maybe then, we'll see that all this pain, all this sacrifice, this . . . shame; maybe then somehow it will seem worth it.

Tony

Today they finally set the trial date. It'll be in another three months. Three more agonizing months of waiting, three more months of not being able to do anything except accumulate more and more debt. Lenny and Bernie say they're going over all of the prosecution's evidence, looking into the histories of all the witnesses, seeing if they can find any more connections between them and Cobb. They say reassuring things to me, but so far they haven't told me anything concrete, anything that might be helpful to our case. They said that when the trial starts, they will be putting in a lot more hours and that I'll need to come up with another fifty to a hundred thousand. A hundred thousand? Fifty thousand? Dollars? Where am I supposed to get that kind of money? We're on food stamps, asshole! Fifty thousand dollars.

What the hell are they smoking, for Christ's sake? I told them that I didn't have a chance in hell of coming up with five thousand, never mind fifty. I'd already given them more than three hundred thousand dollars. "Look," I told them, "Once this is over and I get my license back, I'll be glad to pay you whatever I owe you, but unless you accept food stamps or Medicaid, there's nothing more I can do now. We've already sold most of our furniture. I don't even own a watch any more, for Christ's sake."

"That's fine with us, doctor, if we win. But, if we don't win, then you'll want to appeal and that's going to be very expensive. And there's no guarantee that we'd win that."

"So, what are you saying?"

"Look, Tony," Lenny said, "last week they offered you a plea bargain which you dismissed out of hand. You need to think more about that, about maybe accepting it."

I'll be honest with you. I hadn't thought about it at all. I'd put it right out of my mind as soon as they'd told me about it. They wanted me to plead guilty to a charge of misdemeanor sexual assault and in return, I would only have to serve thirteen months in state prison. If I stuck with my plea of not-guilty, the prosecution would press ahead with the more serious felony sexual assault charges and if I were found guilty, I could end up serving eight years for each charge before having a chance to get out on parole.

If I had been guilty, taking the plea bargain would have been a good deal. But, I was innocent. To accept the deal would mean standing up in court and swearing that I was guilty. And that's not all. The charge that I was supposed to plead guilty to was exposing myself. That was what Toni Fernandez accused me of doing, among other things. Since this was only a misdemeanor, it meant that I could get off with the lighter sentence, whereas any of the felony sexual assault charges carried a minimum federally mandated sentence for each charge of eight years—and there were many charges.

Furthermore, I would have to describe in detail to the judge, for the permanent court record, how and why I'd exposed myself to Ms. Fernandez and express sincere remorse and guilt for what I'd done. Can you imagine it? With my wife and my father and my kids there in court, I'm supposed to swear that yes, I have knowingly and maliciously taken out my dick and asked Ms. Fernandez to perform fellatio and then lied to you all when I claimed that I was innocent.

And, once I've done that—humiliated myself and my family by swearing my guilt—I would forever after be prohibited from claiming otherwise. In other words, I couldn't just accept the deal and then afterwards say, no, I was really innocent, I only said that I'd done it to avoid spending twenty years or more in prison getting my ass reamed. No sir. If I ever did that, it would be a violation of the plea agreement and I would automatically be imprisoned for the entire sentence that I'd been trying to avoid. Once I swore an oath that I was guilty, I was forever guilty. I could never undo it. My kids would have a sex offender for a father for the rest of their lives. And that's not all. No. Once I'd sworn that I was in fact guilty, I would have to register under Megan's Law as a sex offender. Where ever I lived from then on, everyone would know that I was a convicted sex offender. Well, you can understand that there was no way I could do that. No way I was going to claim I was guilty of something I didn't do and then have it shame me and my family and hang over my head for the rest of my life. No way.

Aristeo

I received another letter from Tony. In it, he wrote that he would be going to trial soon and that his lawyers were asking for another fifty thousand dollars. He described how he and Laura and their three children were living with his mother-in-law and were receiving welfare and food stamps from the government. Laura was working as a substitute teacher, but that was only sporadic and nothing they could count on. He asked me if I could loan him some more money. He was facing decades in the state prison. Tony, my friend, a convict? I couldn't bare to think about it. I shared the letter with Alma, of course. She's my wife and also a physician and, as you know, we all went to school together. I was surprised that her initial reaction was anger. More than anger, rage even. She was furious that he had allowed this to happen to him, that he had put this kind of unimaginable burden on his family. It was as if she assumed that he was guilty—if not of the actual complaints, then—of something. I was shocked that she didn't leap to his defense. After all, they had been involved at one time; not lovers, exactly, but romantically interested in each other. Yes, maybe sexually interested as well. After all, we were all young then and full of juice. So, I assumed that she would defend him and be angry at the unfair and unjust way he'd been treated.

"Bullshit," she said. "He's a physician. He had the same training as we did. He knew better. If he'd conducted himself properly, this would never have happened. Do you think it could happen to you? Or to me?"

Of course, I had to say no. On the other hand, if one of my patients claimed that I'd sexually assaulted her in my office, how could I prove otherwise? It's not like there's a witness to what happens during a psychoanalytic hour. I don't record my sessions. How could I prove my innocence? I sent Tony another check for ten thousand dollars and told him that Alma and I were rooting for him. Well, I was and I think, down deep, Alma was too. We both still cared for him very much.

Tony

Today, Lenny and Bernie telephoned and asked me to come to their office. Of course, now, I had very mixed feelings about having a conference with them. At six hundred dollars an hour, I'd rather avoid it. But Lenny was persistent, so I went. I took the bus downtown to their office. We try not to use the car more than we have to. The bottom line is this: as of the end of the month—that is, in another three weeks—they won't continue to be my attorneys of record unless I come up with the fifty thousand they'd asked for. How do you like that? I had thought Lenny was my friend, that he was defending me not only for the fee, but because he knew me and knew what kind of person I was. I believed that he was defending me because he knew that I was innocent. Well, so much for friendship. It all comes down to bucks, doesn't it?

"So, what am I supposed to do? I told you both, we don't have a dime. Laura is shopping with food stamps for Christ's sake. The kids collect empty bottles for the deposit, cut grass, deliver newspapers. You want my kids to come up with your fucking fifty grand?'

"We're not saying that, Tony . . ."

"Fuck you, Lenny. And you too, Bernie. I've given you guys every fucking nickel I had. You've already got it all. Everything! You've got the money from my savings, from the sale of my house and our cars. You've got it all, every dime. And now that I'm completely broke, you're dumping me? Fuck you, the two of you."

Bernie stood up and took a step toward me, then sat down on the edge of the desk and combed his fingers through his hair. "I understand how you feel, doctor, but we've got expenses too. We have overhead, professional liability insurance. We have to pay our investigators, our paralegals, our secretarial staff. And we have our own mortgages and car payments and kids' tuitions. We're victims of cash flow same as you. I hope you realize that we've done everything humanly possible and would continue to do so if we could, but we can't. It's strictly a business decision. Nothing personal."

"Well, Bernie, it's personal to me. In medicine we have our ethical principles and one of them is that the welfare of the patient always comes first and it's unethical to abandon a patient in the middle of their treatment. You see it through if it's at all possible."

"That's just it, doctor. It's not possible. Not beyond the end of this month."

"Then what do you suggest I do? Kill myself?"

"Heaven forbid," Lenny said. "No, you have two alternatives. One, you continue to fight this and accept the services of a court-appointed defense attorney who will handle your case and be paid by the court. Naturally, in that case, we'd share all of our material with whoever it is. The other alternative is to take their plea-bargain as long as it's still available."

That was it. That's what all of this has come down to: a court-appointed defense attorney who is working for something equivalent to minimum wage, or plead guilty to a lesser charge of sexual assault. If I chose to go with the public defender, I'd almost certainly lose. Hell, even Lenny and Bernie, with all their resources weren't all that confident of winning. In fact, now that I think of it, that might have been a big part of their decision to bail out; that they didn't think they could win and didn't want a loss fucking up their record. So, I could go with some bozo from the public defender's office and lose and spend the next fifty or sixty years in prison; or I could plead guilty to something I didn't do and go to jail for *only* thirteen months. Big choice. Maybe I did want to kill myself. After I killed Lenny and Bernie. And Billy Cobb. But, shit, we stopped paying the premiums on my life insurance, so I don't even have that any more. Is all this really happening?

Laura

Tony told me about his conversation with the lawyers. I think I was in shock. Maybe I still am. Their message was clear, even though they didn't come right out and tell him to swallow his pride and take the deal, that's what they were saying. It was clear to me that they were telling him that if he chose to go to trial, he was going to be found guilty. Maybe what I heard was that they were telling him he was guilty. I don't know. I can't even think any more. Tony is such an idealist and has this naïve, boyish optimism that everything will work out, that the truth will win out. I'm not so optimistic. Eight women. Eight women, six of whom have no ulterior motives, believe he used them for his own sexual gratification. How is any jury going to overcome that and find him not guilty? And then he'll be in prison for decades, essentially for the rest of his life. I'm thirty-nine now. By the time he gets out, I'll be an old lady. What am I supposed to do, wait for him? And the kids; Mia is ten. She'll probably have grandchildren of her own. What kind of role is he supposed to play in her life? Is she supposed to tell her children that grandpa is in prison for sexually molesting his women patients? No, if we're going to have any chance at any life together, he's got to take that deal.

Betty

Laura confided in me. She told me what their lawyers did to Tony: dropping him like a hot potato and suggesting that he plead guilty to a lesser charge and serve only a year or so. She doesn't know if he'll do it. Well, he can be stubborn. He never would have completed medical school if he hadn't been stubborn. Either way, what does he have left? His career is ruined whatever he does. Even if he goes to trial and is found not guilty, his career is over, at least here in Clarksburg. I know I could never recommend any of my friends to him after this. Could you? I mean, come on. Eight women claiming the same thing? You can't tell me he didn't do anything. He must have done something. Eight!

Personally—I'll be honest with you—I hope he goes to trial and lets the public defender do his best. Let them find him guilty and send him away for the rest of his life. Then, maybe Laura will be able to let him go and get on with her own life. It'll be better for her and the children to put all this behind them. Lock him up, throw away the key, and let them get on with their lives.

Al

Tony has been talking to me about what he should do. What can I tell him? A decision like that: plead guilty to something you didn't do and have the shame of it for the rest of your life, or take a chance on the trial with a new lawyer. If it were me, I don't know what I'd do. How can you get up in a courtroom and say how and why you did something so terrible—especially if you didn't do it—just to escape a worse punishment, maybe spending the rest of your life in prison. I think, either way you're in prison. You live the rest of your life with that stigma, everyone looking at you and thinking that you're some kind of pervert. Your life is over. He'll never practice again. Not here, anyway. Maybe not anywhere, ever again.

I tell you, I'm just heartbroken over this. I'm sixty-five years old and I'm heartbroken over my kid. I don't know what to think. I can't believe that my son did this. It doesn't seem possible. And yet, there are these women. And the grand jury; those people didn't have any ax to grind with Tony. Why would they go ahead and indict him unless they had some reason to believe that he was guilty? I don't know. I keep going round and round in my head. Thank god for Shirley. She keeps me sane. Still, whenever I think about it, I feel like I've been kicked in the stomach. It's sickening. I didn't work hard my whole life for this, to have my son accused of molesting women. I don't know. I don't know what to think. That's what I ended up telling Tony: "I don't know what to tell you. It's impossible for me to think clearly about this. I'm sorry, but I don't know what to say. I'm sorry I can't help you with this and make it all go away." I feel like throwing up my hands, but how can I forsake him? He's my only son.

Jennifer

·   I've got one more year of high school to get through and I don't know how I'm going to do it. Nobody ever says anything directly to me, but I feel like it's always there, right behind their eyes, waiting in their lungs, for an opportunity to jump out. I wish we had relatives who lived someplace else, any place, maybe in a foreign country, where I could go and live this next year. I hear Mom and Dad arguing about whether he should take the plea bargain. My God, either way it's terrible. Either way people will say he's guilty, whether a jury finds him guilty or he says he's guilty. Everybody says he must be guilty. Either way, I'm going to have a convict for a father. A convicted sex offender. I wish I could get away to college now, someplace away from here, out of the state, where no one knows the name, Cappeletti.

But, if I don't get a scholarship or a Pell Grant, how am I going to be able to afford college? All our money has gone to those damned lawyers. Goddamned bloodsuckers. They should be in jail for robbery. Every dollar that the family had, even the money grandma and grandpa had, has gone to the lawyers. And Daddy is still going to end up in prison. And me, what's going to happen to me? Instead of going to college and becoming a biologist, I'll probably end up waitressing down near the Falls or out at Hiram's. Christ! Sometimes I wish I were dead. Sometimes . . . I wish he were.

Tony

It's come down to this. Tomorrow morning I have to decide whether to make the switch to the public defender and go to trial and risk being found guilty and sentenced to fifty years or more; or to take the plea bargain offered by the state and plead guilty to exposing myself and serve thirteen months. Lenny and Bernie (the bastards) have made it clear that the smart thing to do would be to take the plea bargain. For them, the issue of guilt or innocence is irrelevant. It's a matter of cutting your losses. Part of me knows that. I understand the rationality of that. It's just that it's so degrading, so humiliating. But, the idea of spending all those years in prison . . . it's incomprehensible. How could I possibly survive that? I'll tell you the truth. It scares the hell out of me. I'm forty-two years old. I'm not a young kid any more. I'm not an athlete like I was twenty years ago when I could take care of myself. I'm not in shape. How am I going to be able to defend myself against those guys? I can't do it. I can't. Thirteen months is bad enough, but the rest of my life? I can't do it. When it comes right down to it, those bastards haven't left me any choice. I've got to take their fucking deal, got to stand up in court and say I'm guilty. I don't know how I'm going to do that either, but I'm going to have to find a way. I'll have to, that's all. I just have to find a way.

Casey

Tonight Dad called us all into Grandma's living room. All of us, even Grandpa and Shirley and Mia were there. He had tears in his eyes and he kept choking up, telling us what he was going to do tomorrow. Mom tried to be consoling, sitting next to him on the sofa with her arm around him and patting him like he was a baby. But, the rest of us were quiet, except for Mia, who was crying. Grandma held her and tried to comfort her. I felt awful. I felt ashamed that my father was going to go to prison. He was going to be a convict. I've heard the saying, "like father, like son." In the past, it made me feel good, like it was some kind of guarantee that I'd be successful, maybe a doctor like him. I used to be so proud of him. Now, I wonder if it means that I'm going to fuck up my life too by doing something bad. It's scary. It makes me think, "What's going to happen to me? What kind of person am I going to grow up to be?" Shit, I'm only a freshman in high school. Am I going to end up in prison too?

I mean, if I had the chance to look at pussy all day long, I'd probably do something too. Dad says that it's different when you're a doctor, it's not anything that's sexually exciting. It's like looking at somebody's elbows or kneecaps. I don't know if I buy that. I mean, how can you not get sexually excited if you're staring right into pussy or feeling breasts? Christ, I have a hardon all the time as it is and I never even get to see the real thing. So, of course I think he's guilty. How could he not be? I'd be guilty if it were me. I mean, how can you not be? It's like saying that if you came across a bag of money in the street, you wouldn't pick it up. Bullshit. So, my attitude is, yeah, he probably did it, and that all doctors probably do it. Shit, even priests are doing it. He just happened to get caught because the sheriff has it out for him, that's all. That's the only difference. So, shit, I think what he did was normal and I'd probably have done it too and it's plain unfair that he has to spend time in jail for it. But, he's my dad and he's a good guy and I'm sticking with him. And whatever happens, happens. In a year he'll be out and we'll be together again and it'll all be behind us. And anytime anybody even thinks of saying anything about it to me, they'll end up with a fat lip or a busted nose 'cause I'm not taking any shit from anybody.

Shirley

When the kids came over this morning, they knew that their parents were going to court with Al and Betty, and that their father would be accepting the plea bargain. They realized that he didn't want them there hearing him swear that he was guilty of committing any of the crimes that he was accused of. They were aware that the judge had agreed to a sentence of thirteen months in exchange for their father's guilty plea. And they understood that he felt he had to take the plea bargain, in spite of swearing his innocence, in order to avoid the almost certain consequences of being found guilty of all charges and possibly spending the rest of his life in prison. They all said their tearful goodbyes to him before they left their house, believing that they might not see him again until they visited him in jail.

Casey didn't want to talk and withdrew into one of his computer games. But, Mia kept close to Jennifer and me and we talked a little bit about how sad she felt and speculated as to why so many people would lie about her father. I had no answers for her. Jennifer was just as confused as Mia was, but she was also more angry at the injustice of it all. I had no answers for her either. When Al tried to find some rational explanation of why it was all happening, there were no answers to be found. I end up feeling completely helpless. All I can do is nod my head and pat their arm. What can I say? All I can do is let them know I love them and feel for them. But, that seems so pitifully inadequate.

Betty

This morning, we went to court. Tony and Laura were adamant about not wanting any of the kids there, so they stayed at Alberto's house with Shirley, while Al and I accompanied Laura and Tony to the courthouse. Tony had finally agreed to take the plea bargain and Lenny graciously agreed to represent him without charging him anything extra. He's all heart. There weren't many people in the courtroom: a few reporters, some of the women who had accused Tony, and some curiosity seekers. We found seats behind the railing that separated us from Tony and Lenny, who were seated at one table in front of us. The prosecutor and two of his assistants sat at the other table, talking among themselves while the bailiff and the court reporter chatted with each other. We waited. The judge was late. I was nervous and I'm sure everyone else was too; not that there was any suspense about what was going to happen. Tony had told us about the script that he was to follow and we knew pretty much what he would say and what his sentence would be. Finally, the judge came in and we all stood up when we were told to and sat down again when told to, just like in church. The judge began by saying that he understood that Dr. Cappeletti wanted to change his plea. Was that correct? Lenny got up and started to say, "That's correct, your honor . . ." and then Tony grabbed his arm and shook his head. Then he stood up as well and said, "No, your honor. I have given the offer of a plea bargain considerable thought and, I'm sorry, but I cannot swear here in court that I am guilty of committing any crime. Therefore, I do not want to change my plea of not guilty."

As you can imagine, we were all in shock. Everybody. Stunned. Laura screamed out, "NO!" before I could stop her. I had to hold her down. She was furious. If she'd had a gun, I think she might have shot him right there on the spot. He had given in to all of her pleading about how they needed him to come home as soon as possible, how they could not manage without him, that he couldn't risk the almost certainty of being found guilty at a trial and spending the rest of his life in prison. He had agreed, finally, and promised her that he'd plead guilty and take the shorter sentence. And now here he was, throwing those promises away as easily as a gum wrapper.

I was furious too, but mostly for Laura's sake. As I may have mentioned, I secretly thought she and the kids would be better off if they went on with their lives without him. Still, I was as surprised as anyone and thought, "That selfish bastard. He's thinking only of himself, of his pride, his reputation. He's not thinking of his responsibility as a husband or as a father. I knew it.

That self-centered sonofabitch." I held onto Laura, consoling her, restraining her, letting her know that I was one with her.

I knew there was an uproar going on around me; the voices of the lawyers, the judge, shouting, the gavel banging, but I was focused totally on Laura. Then I became aware of Alberto. He sat slumped in his seat, in shock like the rest of us. I reached across Laura to touch his arm. He looked at me, his lips pressed tightly together and the muscles of his clenched jaw working. I saw the confusion in his eyes. He was stunned. He didn't understand how his son could do this, nor why. Why was Tony being so self-destructive? The next thing I knew the commotion, the hubbub, had quieted down and the judge was setting the starting date for the trial for the following month, for the Tuesday after Labor Day, September 6, 2011. Then the prosecutor asked that Tony be incarcerated while awaiting trial. Lenny objected and the judge agreed to let Tony remain out on bail. Then we all left. Lenny shook his head as he patted Tony on the shoulder and told him to get in touch with his new attorney at the public defender's office. And then, the four of us: me, Laura, Tony, and Alberto, were left standing in the parking lot. Tony was full of apologies for disappointing everyone. Laura was so angry, she couldn't look at him. Al looked skyward, as if seeking divine direction. He couldn't comprehend what had just happened nor why. He had no idea what to do: whether to be supportive or whether to whack Tony one for being a selfish asshole.

Well, I thought, soon there will be a trial and he'll be found guilty and then Laura and the kids will be with me and we'll all start a new life together. I felt like a pioneer woman, pulling up stakes and moving West, only I wouldn't be moving. And Tony, he'd be starting a new life too. Part of me felt validated in an I-told-you-so kind of way. But, mostly I felt sorry for Laura and the kids, not for him. He brought all this down on himself. Of course he did; and on his father and wife and children too. I don't care how many times he gets himself raped while he's in jail, he'll never get an ounce of pity out of me.

Tony

The four of us drove back to Betty's house in silence. I knew I had to explain why I had changed my mind, why I had disappointed them; but I thought it would be better to wait until we were all sitting down in the house so we could talk at length, without feeling rushed. Laura sat beside me while I drove, but she kept her face averted, looking out her window. I saw Betty in the rearview mirror trying to comfort my father. It was obvious that Pop didn't understand why I'd done what I did. When I pulled up into the driveway and stopped the van, Laura jumped out and slammed the door behind her. I looked at Betty and my father, but neither one of them would look at me. Each of us marched silently into the house like we were going to a funeral.

Betty
"I don't know about anyone else, but I need a drink."

Laura
"Make one for me too, Mom."

Tony
"I'll have one too, if you don't mind."

Betty
"Help yourself. You know where everything is. How about you, Al? Can I make you a drink?"

Al
"Yes, thank you, Betty. Whatever you're having will be fine."

Tony
"Listen, I know that I owe you all an explanation . . ."

Laura

"An explanation? You just fucking abandoned us and you talk about an *explanation*? You threw us away, threw your family away, and you're going to explain?"

Tony

"What would you call it? Look, I know I surprised all of you. I surprised myself. I didn't plan it this way . . ."

Laura

"No? How did you plan it? What other goddamned surprises do you have in store for us?"

Tony

"Nothing. I don't have any surprises . . ."

Betty

(Handing a drink to Al and to Laura, then taking one for herself and sitting down) "Well, that would be nice for a change."

Al

"You couldn't have been as surprised as we were. Just last night, Tony, you sat here in this very room and promised Laura, and the rest of us, that you would take the plea bargain. You agreed that it was the best thing to do for your family, your kids, Laura; even for Betty, and for me and Shirley. Now you decide all of a sudden to put us through the farce and public shame of a trial? For what? You know how it'll end. We all know how this is going to end. I don't understand. Why? Why did you do this?"

Tony

"I know. I had every intention of going through with it. I did. But, once we got into the courtroom, I felt myself tensing up. I don't know what it was exactly: fear, revulsion, anger, whatever, but I felt myself going rigid, almost as if I were digging in my heels, resisting being pulled into something that was no good for me. All

I knew was that the idea of letting those words come out of my mouth seemed disgusting to me. Revolting. I actually felt sick and thought that I might vomit. And I realized that I couldn't do it. Physically. I just couldn't go through with it. Swearing to those lies, saying that I'd exposed myself to that bitch. I know it doesn't seem fair to you all, but no one has a right to make me say those things. Going to prison scares the hell out of me. God knows it does. But, as bad as it may be, I'd rather do that than swear in court that I was guilty of any of those charges of molesting my patients."

Al

"You don't know what you're saying. You've got some half-assed idea in your head about being some kind of martyr, sacrificing yourself on the alter of truth. That's stupid, Tony. Look at me. Open your eyes. You're going to go to a state prison for fifty or sixty years, depending on how vile the judge thinks you are. Truth has nothing to do with it. This isn't about guilt or innocence or your reputation. All of that's lost already. This is about the reality of the rest of your life. Don't be an idiot. Your mother and I didn't raise you to be a fool."

Betty

"He thinks he's Don Quixote. He thinks he's going to be a hero in a romantic fantasy."

Tony

"That's not true. I just can't imagine standing up in that courtroom and saying those words, fabricating a whole make-believe tale of being some kind of sex-crazed nut and swearing that it's true. And it's not fair that you should try to make me do that."

Laura

"Not fair? You think it's fair what you have put all of us through for these past sixteen months? And what we're all going to suffer through for the rest of our lives because of you? You think that's fair?"

Betty

"Tony, do you have any idea of how goddamned selfish you're being? You're thinking only of yourself. Like your father said, it's too late for you to be concerned with how this is going to make you look, with what people might think of you. That's already done. Everyone already thinks you're a guilty prick as charged. So why don't you do your family a favor and just own up to it?"

Tony

"Is that true? Do you all think that I'm guilty?"

Al

"Betty didn't mean us. She meant the town, the people we know . . ."

Tony

"Do you believe I'm guilty?"

Al

"No, of course not. But, Betty's right, Tony. It's no use trying to preserve your reputation. Going through a trial, even if by some miracle you were to win, it wouldn't change anybody's mind. In their eyes you're guilty, regardless of whether you go to trial or not, regardless of what you say in court."

Tony

"Laura, do you believe I'm guilty, too?"

Laura

"Tony, I don't know what to believe. I wasn't there. I don't know."

Tony

"You don't know? You mean you actually think it's possible that I did any of those things?"

Laura

"You're a man, aren't you? Of course it's possible."

Tony

"I don't believe this. I can't believe what I'm hearing. We've been married for eighteen years and you actually believe that it's possible that I molested those women? You have so little faith in me? I thought you loved me, Laura. How could you?"

Betty

"Wait a minute, Tony. This isn't about Laura. This is about you, just you."

Laura

"Tony, I do have faith in you . . . about some things. But belief means being without doubt. Without a doubt, I know God exists. But, when it comes to this, I do have some doubt. I'm not saying that I think you're guilty. I'm not saying that. What I'm saying—and I realize that I've never said this out loud before—is that I have doubts. I can't say for certain that you couldn't have done these things. I just can't."

Tony

"Thank you very much for your undying commitment and vote of confidence. Does that go for the rest of you too? Do each of you doubt that I'm innocent? Doesn't one of you know who I am? Don't you *know* that I am incapable of having done what I've been accused of?"

Al

"Tony, we all love you . . ."

Tony

"Oh, Pop, that's not the issue. Although maybe it is. What I'm saying—and I see it clearly now on all your faces—is that each of you has some doubt as to whether I'm guilty or not. None of you is willing to say, 'Even though I wasn't there and have no proof, I know without a shadow of a doubt that he couldn't have done it. It's impossible. Just plain fucking impossible.' And none of you can do that, can you? None of you.

"Holy Christ. None of you completely believes in me and yet you've got the gall to say that I'm selfish and that I should . . . shit on myself in public. For you. Fuck you. How can you even bear to look at me if you think I'm guilty of this crap?"

Betty

"Now we're the guilty ones. Jesus, Tony, you never cease to amaze me."

Laura

"No, Mom, give him a break. Tony, please don't confuse the two. Like your dad said, we all love you. We do. But don't confuse that with our having doubts. How could we not have doubts? You're not a saint. Don't say you've never looked at another woman, never had any sexual fantasies about another woman."

Tony

"As a man, not as a doctor . . ."

Laura

"You're human. You're not perfect. I know you're not perfect and nobody expects you to be. So, if eight women accuse you of something, don't blame us for having doubts. Of course we have doubts. How could we be absolutely certain?"

Tony

"Because I thought that you knew me better than that. If you really knew me, you would know I couldn't do anything like that."

Betty

"Tony, why shouldn't we think it's possible? My husband loved me. I know he did. But, he flirted with other women. And we all know that some women fall in love with their doctors, with their obstetricians, their pediatricians, whatever. Are you telling us that it's impossible for you to be tempted by a beautiful naked woman in front of you who gazes up at you with loving admiration? Who could resist that?"

Tony

"That's your fantasy, Betty. Not mine. That's not how it is at all."

Al

"Maybe not, Tony. But none of us are physicians. We can only imagine what it's like, based on our own perspectives. I know that I've sometimes wondered what it's like for you, a young handsome gifted doctor; I would think it has to be tempting sometimes . . ."

Tony

"Jesus, even you, Pop. The thing that none of you realize is that for a physician it really is different. You're not looking at something sexual. You're looking at a body part. You're looking for signs, evidence of some disease, something wrong . . ."

Laura

"Bullshit, Tony. You've told me yourself that probably ten percent of all professionals: doctors, lawyers, therapists—all get sexually involved with their patients, or clients or whatever. So don't try to tell us that a physician is some saintly being, without human flaws, incapable of fucking their patients."

Tony

"Jesus, Laura. Are you now accusing me of fucking my patients?"

Laura

"Stop being so damned defensive. I'm only saying that you yourself told me about physicians who've been found guilty of having sex with their patients and lost their licenses as a result."

Tony

"So? That's somebody else. That's not me."

Al

"Tony, Laura is simply making the point that it's not above every physician to get involved with their patients. Not every physician looks only at 'body parts' and doesn't see a beautiful breast and a sexy behind."

Tony

"Okay, maybe not every physician. But, we're talking about me. Me! Not somebody else. And I'm . . . really pissed. I can't believe it, that none of you knows me. How could you believe that of me? It's like everything is suddenly unreal, like my whole life has been a lie or a dream. What I thought was true, what I thought was real, wasn't. It never was. I thought I knew you, but I don't. I never did. I feel like I'm going crazy. I don't know what's true or real and what's not. I can't trust . . . my own perception, my own thinking, my own conclusions. Nothing is real any more."

Laura

"Tony, I don't think you're listening to us."

Betty

"The poor boy."
Tony gets up from his chair and walks out of the front door.

Al

"Tony, where are you going?"

Tony

"I don't know; I've just got to . . ."

Laura

"Tony, come back. Don't leave."

Betty

"Let him go, Laura. He's got to lick his wounds. He'll be back."

Al

"Christ, what a mess. I'm just glad the kids aren't here."

Betty

"Maybe you should give Shirley a call and let her know what's happened. She's probably wondering why she hasn't heard from us and is worrying her head off."

Laura

"Yes, and the kids must be worrying too."

Tony

When I left the house, I had no idea where I was going. I jumped into the van knowing only that I had to get away from the house. That's what I really wanted: to get away; to escape the horrible shock of rejection, the hurt, the anger. I wanted to turn my back on them, reject them, hurt them. I was outraged that they, my family, my wife and father, could turn on me like that. I started driving north and after a while, headed up Fairfax Mountain. Near the top, there's a lookout where you can park. That's where Laura and I used to go before we were married. I parked the van and walked down one of the paths and found a place to sit down and look out over the valley.

Down there, that's where I grew up, went to school, played baseball, went to college, met my wife, raised my kids, and enjoyed a thriving medical practice. From up here, it all seemed so peaceful. Even downtown Clarksburg, with its big office buildings and small factories, appeared quaint and picturesque from up here. I reflected back on a wonderful life. I don't know how it could have been any better. Everything worked out for me. I got everything I'd ever wanted. It had been a life that kids dream about and wish for. And I'd actually lived it.

And now . . . now it seems that everything has turned to shit, as if a giant monster has reached down and plucked me up and, before I could do anything, squeezed the life out of me. All of a sudden, just like that, everything I had was gone. Shut your eyes and quick as that, it all disappeared. Is life anything more than a dream? It seems that ephemeral, illusory. Right now, everything I'd always believed in seems wrong. How could I have been so mistaken about such a basic thing as how my own father or my own wife felt about me?

Then I thought of what had taken place this morning in the courtroom. How did it happen? How did it come to this, my having to choose between confessing to the misdemeanor of exposing myself and going to trial to defend myself against a flood of serious sexual felonies? Originally, I thought it was all about the law suit in which I'd have testified against Billy Cobb and the machinations he engaged in to sabotage my testimony against him by destroying me. That would explain his girlfriend and her girlfriend's involvement, but not the others. I don't understand the how of it or the why. It's like, for no good reason, God simply decided to test me. So, if that's true, what should I do?

I can't take the plea bargain. Dad and Laura think it's about my trying to save my reputation. Ha! That's a laugh. What reputation? As they said, my reputation is already shot to hell. No, they don't understand. Physically, I can't get myself to do it. Being in that court room in front of the judge, I realized that it was no longer some abstract thing we were talking about. This was tangible; it was the actual feel of the words in my mouth. It was not only a betrayal of myself, but also a betrayal of everything I believed in. It wasn't right to let them or the system manipulate me like that and force me to betray myself. It's not right.

Yes, I know that it probably means that I'm going to go to prison for a long time, a very long time. And, yes, I know that it's going to be tough on all of them, especially the kids. And, to tell you the truth, I don't know if I'll be able to do it myself. I don't. It scares the shit out of me. But, maybe if there's a trial and those women have to get up on the stand and be subjected to a cross examination, maybe they'll recant their stories. Maybe I won't be found guilty. Maybe I'll get off. Why not? There's always a chance. If I believe, who knows? Maybe I'll get off. It's possible. I mean, a public defender lawyer is still a lawyer, isn't he? Just because he's working for peanuts doesn't mean he's stupid, right? So, maybe it's not stupid for me to stick to my guns. Everybody is assuming that the sheer number of women who are accusing me is in itself an insurmountable obstacle. But, what if it's all a house of cards, all built on a flimsy foundation, something that really can't stand up to any kind of scrutiny? Why is everyone being so pessimistic? I can beat this thing. I know it. I've just got to persist, to stand up for myself no matter what, even if everyone else is ready to give up. I can't. I won't.

Al

Laura and I went to the courtroom every day and sat behind Tony and his young public defender; bright, but still a kid really, just out of Temple law school, named Tommy Grant. Grant was still young enough to be hopeful and idealistic and I have to give him credit; he put all he had into defending Tony. The judge was a no-nonsense woman who seemed to be annoyed that Tony had elected to go to trial and, consequently, she didn't cut Grant any slack. For example, when the prosecution was finished with the testimony of Linda Davidson, Billy Cobb's mistress, Grant tried to bring out that relationship in his cross examination, but Judge Eiswerth sustained one of an endless stream of objections from the prosecution and ruled Tommy's line of questioning irrelevant.

However, he was able to undermine the credibility of a couple of Tony's accusers. For example, Mrs. Jable had claimed that Tony had given her an unnecessary and lengthy pelvic examination and in the process had deliberately stimulated her genitals. Tommy was able to point out that Dr. Cappeletti's medical records showed that she had been a patient of his for seven years and that she had asked him to conduct a gynecological examination as part of her yearly physical every year for that entire period. Yes, she agreed that was so. So, Grant pursued, given that she herself had requested that Dr. Cappeletti perform this exam instead of her going to a gynecologist, the exam had not been done capriciously, but was a routine part of her annual examination. But, she insisted, he was stimulating her sexually instead of just conducting the exam. Had she felt that way at the time? Well, she had been extremely uncomfortable. Still, Tommy continued, most women experience physical and psychological discomfort during such an examination. If she felt that he was taking advantage of her, then why did she continue to have him conduct his examination annually for seven years? And why hadn't she said anything about this to anyone before? Well, she said, she wasn't sure that he was doing something that he shouldn't and didn't want to cause any trouble. And when was it, Tommy asked, that she first began to think that Dr. Cappeletti had done something wrong? Was it after the detectives told her that other women had come forward and accused him? And hadn't those very same detectives suggested to her that perhaps she too, had been an unknowing victim? Yes, she reluctantly agreed, that probably was when she realized that her discomfort might be a result of his doing something he shouldn't have.

Grant was able to elicit this kind of admission from a another of the state's witnesses, Mrs. Peck, though not any of the others. The others stuck to their guns and refused to admit that they had been manipulated or pressured by the detectives or the prosecutor's office. Still, Laura and I thought that he had done a good job of planting some doubt in the jurors' minds. As a result, I began to feel hopeful and have a little confidence that my son would be proven innocent.

Laura

Tony begged me to attend the trial every day, even though it meant my not working. And the fact was, we needed every dime and nickel we could lay our hands on. Besides, I was so furious with him for not taking the plea bargain that it galled me to have to admit that it would look terrible for him if I wasn't there to be supportive. When I saw Tommy Grant, my heart just sank. He looked like he was nineteen years old; short, skinny, red haired and freckled. Tommy—I still can't get used to calling him *Mister* Grant—started off slowly, but by the time the jury selection was over and the actual trial had started, I saw that he was beginning to gain some confidence.

I played the dutiful wife and smiled when I was supposed to and made sure to dress modestly. I think that Al's and my presence there in the courtroom everyday helped to soften the image of Tony as a sexual predator and to remind the good people of Clarksburg of the wonderful reputation Tony had always enjoyed in the community ever since he'd been a boy. But, in spite of this display of true-blue family love and apple-pie virtues, privately I held onto my anger at Tony for putting all of us through this ordeal of public censure and humiliation; not to mention the pain of his almost certainly spending decades in a state prison.

In contrast to Tommy Grant's vulnerable and innocent appearance (and also his boyish enthusiasm which, I am sure, endeared him to others as well as myself), the prosecutor was a longtime political insider, an old warhorse named Howard Dennis Sullivan. Mr. Sullivan was a big man, tall, with a large frame. He had probably played football in college and was likeable enough to become a fixture in local politics. And he appeared to be on friendly terms with all of the employees assigned to the courtroom. He was a longtime crony of Sheriff Cobb. After all these years in the local spotlight, Mr. Sullivan had assumed the role in the courtroom of Lord of the Manor. This was his territory and everyone was here solely as a consequence of his gracious invitation. He strode comfortably back and forth in front of the jury and the judge with an air of confidence and dealt with the jury and female witnesses in what I thought was a patronizing, manner. I took an instant dislike to him and imagined that the rest of the women in the courtroom, including the eight women jurors and Judge Eiswerth, might have felt the same way about him. Of course I hated him. And feared him as well. From my perspective Mr. Sullivan was the enemy, the person who was threatening to take my husband away from me. And he was politically powerful enough and experienced enough to do it.

In contrast, Tommy Grant appealed to my maternal instincts. I wanted to hold him, and protect him. I felt like cheering whenever he made a point and booing every time Mr. Sullivan was sustained in one of his many objections.

When it came time for Grant to cross examine Toni Fernandez, my stomach was in knots. Tony and I glanced nervously at each other. I was absolutely convinced that she was a complete and total liar. I didn't believe her story for one second and hoped that everyone else in the courtroom was intelligent enough to see the obvious: that she was a psychopathic bitch and lying came as easily to her as breathing. Mr. Sullivan had elicited her testimony in which she charged Tony with performing an unnecessary vaginal exam on her although she had gone to his office with a cough and some congestion. During the course of the examination, she said that Tony had stimulated her in a sexual manner and then exposed his erect penis and asked her to take it in her mouth and suck it.

Tommy Grant picked up a folder which I recognized as containing a report from Lenny's investigator and started his cross examination by asking her age and address, occupation, and marital status.[1] She admitted to being fifty-two, twice-divorced and

---

[1] The following account of the cross examination of Ms. Fernandez does not include most of the innumerable objections, usually sustained, which were made by Mr. Sullivan.

living in an apartment complex on the eastern edge of Clarksburg. Currently, she said, she worked as a nurse's aide in a nursing home in town.

"And you went to see Dr. Cappeletti for some lung congestion and a cough, is that right?"

"That's right."

"And this was the first time you had consulted Dr. Cappeletti?"

"Yes, and it was the only time."

"And why was it that you sought him out?"

"Because I was congested, like I said. I was concerned that maybe I had pneumonia."

"I'm sorry, Ms. Fernandez, what I meant was, why did you decide to see Dr. Cappeletti when you had never gone to his office before? Why him and not some other doctor?"

"I don't know. I heard he was good, so I thought I'd try him out."

"You didn't have a physician of your own? Someone you saw regularly?"

"No."

"But, you've lived in Clarksburg for some time, haven't you? Over twenty years?"

"Yes, I moved here with my first husband, when I was in my twenties."

"I see. And did you have any children by that marriage, Ms. Fernandez?"

"Yes, I had a daughter, Sonia."

"Uh huh, and how old is Sonia now?"

"Uh, let's see, she's almost twenty-seven now."

"She's not living with you now?"

"No, Sonia moved out when she was eighteen."

"I see, and where is she living now?"

"Uh, out west someplace. Oregon, I think. I'm not positive."

"You and Sonia don't keep in close touch with each other?"

"You know kids. You raise them and sacrifice for them and they never appreciate it. They just want to be free to do whatever they want, regardless. I'm sure your mother would understand."

"Here you are, then, having lived here in Clarksburg for over twenty years. You raise your only child here and yet, you don't have a physician you can consult when you are concerned that you might be seriously ill? Suffering from pneumonia? Why is that?"

"I don't know. I don't remember. Maybe my regular physician was busy and I couldn't get an appointment."

"So you did have a regular physician, someone you usually consulted?"

"What I meant was . . ."

"Yes?"

"I guess I meant that there have been doctors I've used in the past. Maybe for a while, I might have used one more or less regularly, but last year, I wasn't using any one doctor as my primary care physician."

"Are you saying that last year you might, in fact, have used a number of different physicians?"

"Yes, that's what I meant."

"And did you visit any of those physicians for the congestion you were concerned about?"

"Uh, no. I only went to Dr. Cappeletti."

"Because someone told you he was a good physician, you said."

"Yes."

"And do you remember who that someone was?"

"No. I don't remember."

"Then, Mrs. Fernandez, let me refresh your memory. Dr. Cappeletti's records show that on the paperwork you filled out, you wrote down Linda Davidson as the person who had referred you to him. Does that sound right?"

"I guess so. I don't remember."

"But, it probably was Mrs. Davidson, given that it was her name you wrote down?"

"Yeah, probably. Sure, if that's what I wrote."

"Then you know Mrs. Davidson?"

"Yes. She's an acquaintance."

"Only an acquaintance? Not what you might call a friend?"

"Okay, yes, a friend. Sure."

"In fact you both live in the same apartment complex, don't you?"

"Yes, we do."

"And you both use the same hair salon?"

"Yes, I think so."

"And are in the same bowling league?"

"Yes, that's true."

"In fact on the same bowling team, isn't that right?"

"Yes."

"And you have gone out together on double dates, is that not correct?"

"Uh, I'm not sure . . ."

"I'm surprised that you don't remember, Mrs. Fernandez. You and Mrs. Davidson have been seen together frequently at the Hilltop Roadhouse on Rt. 53, in the township of Green Hills, which is about twenty miles east of Clarksburg. Does that ring a bell?"

"Now that you mention it, yes, of course I remember."

"Do you remember the names of any of the men who accompanied you there on any of those occasions?"

"Not offhand. They were only casual acquaintances."

"Perhaps so. But, how about the gentleman who accompanied Mrs. Davidson? I understand that Mrs. Davidson was usually in the company of the same gentleman. Do you recall who that was?" (At that point, Mr. Sullivan strongly objected and was sustained. Judge Eiswerth warned Mr. Grant that he had already been cautioned not to pursue that line of questioning. So the jury never got to hear Sheriff Billy Cobb's name brought up in this context. Tommy Grant sighed in frustration and then returned to his cross-examination of Toni Fernandez.)

"Mrs. Fernandez, did Mrs. Davidson ever talk to you about her complaint about Dr. Cappeletti?"

"No, not that I recall."

"No? The two of you never talked about it?"

"I don't think so. Maybe after we both had made complaints, but not before."

"So, let me understand this: you have testified that Mrs. Davidson is a friend of yours. She lives in the same apartment complex. You use the same hairdresser, bowl together regularly on the same bowling team, and have gone out together frequently on double dates; such good friends that when you were ill and lacking a regular physician, she referred you to her own physician, Dr. Cappeletti, whom she had been consulting—without any complaint, I may add—for a number of years. And within one week of your only visit to Dr. Cappeletti, Mrs. Davidson accuses the doctor of sexual improprieties and barely a week later, so do you. And yet you say you never talked about it with her until afterward? Is that accurate? Is that really true?"

"I'm not sure. I don't remember."

"Does that mean that you might have talked with your friend, Linda Davidson, before you made your complaint?"

"I don't remember. We've talked so much since then, I can't remember what might have been said before or what might have been said afterwards."

"So, then it is possible that you and your friend, Linda, might have spoken together about Dr. Cappeletti, about making a complaint against him, before *either* of you actually made the complaint."

"I guess so. Is it possible? Yeah, I guess it's possible."

"Might have compared notes, so to speak?"

"It's possible."

"Discussed the possibility of bringing charges against him?"

"I guess. Yes, it's possible."

"I see. So whose idea was it to bring charges against Dr. Cappeletti? Was it your idea?"

"I don't remember."

"You don't remember whose idea it was to go to the police and file a complaint? To initiate these legal proceedings? I ask you again, Mrs. Fernandez, was it your idea?"

"No, I don't think so. I mean I think each of us thought of it on our own. It was mutual."

"So you both discussed the possibility of going to the authorities and bringing charges against Dr. Cappeletti and decided to do it together."

"Yes, that's how it probably was."

"I see. So, why did you wait for almost a week after your good friend brought charges, before you decided to come forward yourself?"

"I don't know. Maybe I was busy."

"And maybe you thought that it would look more as though you were each acting independently, look less like the conspiracy it was, if some time elapsed between your allegations and those of your good friend. Tell me, whose idea was that? Or did somebody else suggest that to you?" (Howard Sullivan's objections punctuated this cross examination with the regularity of a period at the end of each of Tommy Grant's sentences. Many were sustained, but surprisingly, Judge Eiswerth allowed Grant to maintain his momentum.)

"I don't know that it was anyone's idea. It just happened that way."

"Just happened?"

"Yes."

"No one suggested the idea to you or Mrs. Davidson?"

"No."

"All right. Thank you. Now, let's go back to the reason you consulted Dr. Cappeletti. You said that you were suffering from congestion and were concerned about possible pneumonia."

"Yes, that's correct."

"And are you aware that Dr. Cappeletti's notes for your appointment—your only appointment with him—says that you complained to him of severe neck and back pain from a previous automobile accident and that you requested that he write a prescription for pain medication?"

"Yes. I am aware of that."

"What do you make of the difference between your description of the reason for your visit and Dr. Cappelletti's description?"

"It just shows what a liar he is, the lengths to which he'll go to cover up his outrageous behavior. He's lying, outright lying."

"Of course, when two people have a different memory of what has taken place, it may indeed be because one of them is lying. Sometimes it's very difficult to tell which one might be lying, or perhaps simply mistaken, or maybe misremembering. At any rate, in the absence of corroborating information, sometimes it can be quite difficult to decide who to believe."

"But, I'm not the only one who's saying it, am I? That he's taking advantage of us women? There's others that are saying the same thing."

"Yes, I think we all may have noticed a remarkable similarity in your testimony, especially with that of your friend, Linda—Except for one thing. Are you aware that you are the only complainant to accuse Dr. Cappeletti of exposing himself?"

"Yes, I think so."

"And requesting a sexual act?"

"Yes, I think so."

"Yes, none of the other women who have made complaints have accused Dr. Cappelletti of exposing himself or of requesting any kind of sexual act. Only you. Even your good friend, Linda Davidson, who had been consulting Dr. Cappelletti for years, didn't accuse him of exposing himself to her. Don't you find that interesting?"

"I'm not sure what you mean."

"Well, I find it very interesting that Dr. Cappeletti had been treating all of these other women for considerable periods of time, some for many years. I'm sure that he would have felt much more comfortable with them than with you. This was, after all, the first time he'd met you; it was your first and only visit to his office. Why would he choose you of all people to expose himself to and to make a request for oral sex and not choose anyone else?"

"I don't know. You'd have to ask him."

"I did. I did. And I must say, I agree with his answer; that the very idea of his approaching anyone in the way you described, never mind a fifty-one year old woman who is in his office for the first time, is absolutely ridiculous and totally beyond belief. (Yes, of course, Sullivan objected strenuously and was sustained, but the testimony had been heard.)

"Actually, Mrs. Fernandez, when I asked you before about your explanation of why you chose to consult Dr. Cappeletti, I was thinking of something else. Do you recall the name of the medication you requested from Dr. Cappeletti?"

"It . . . there was no . . . I didn't request any pain medication. I was there for a cough. And he practically raped me . . ."

"Interesting that you refer to it as pain medication. Have you ever had a prescription for Oxycontin?"

"Yes, I have."

"And Oxycodone?"

"Yes."

"And Percocet?"

"Yes."

"Do you recall how long ago it was when you had your first prescription for any of these medications?"

"No."

"I have records here that show that your use of these medications started at least as far back as 1980. Would you say that sounds reasonable?"

"It's possible, yes."

"And would you say that your use of these pain medications has been more or less continuous since then?"

"No, not continuous at all."

"So, there have been periods when you were not taking any of these medications?"

"Yes, of course."

"And how long would you say those periods were? Days? Weeks? Months?"

"Long periods. I don't remember. I didn't keep track."

"No? You didn't keep track? But weren't you in treatment for addiction to these pain medications?"

"Yes. And I was cured."

"Yes you were. Apparently many times. Our records show—and I am confident they are not complete—that you have been in drug rehabilitation both as an inpatient and as an outpatient, on at least four occasions during the past thirty years. It was recommended that you obtain outpatient drug counseling and attend Narcotics Anonymous meetings when you were discharged from each of those treatment facilities. Is that not correct?"

"Yes."

"So, Dr. Cappeletti could not have known of the details of your history of drug addiction when he saw you for the first time last year. The truth is that you went to him because all the other physicians you had consulted over the last thirty years knew of your drug problem and refused to write any more prescriptions for you. Your close friend, Linda, told you about her doctor, one she had been using confidently for years, and suggested that because he was so caring, he might be an easy mark for you. And when Dr. Cappeletti astutely suspected that you had a drug problem, he did what any good, competent, ethical physician would do: he refused to write your prescription. And you left his office frustrated and angry. Isn't that what happened, Ms. Fernandez?"

"No. I went to see him because I was sick and he took advantage of me. He's a sick whacko."

"Mrs. Fernandez, in your scheme of things, I'm sure all of your problems are the result of other people being sick whackos. That's all."

Al

Sitting next to Laura in the court room every day, was one of the most difficult things I've ever done. On one hand, my son was being accused of betraying his oath, his medical ethics, and taking advantage of his position of trust and authority for his own sexual gratification. Although I had reluctantly come to the conclusion that there might have been some possibility that he had done these things, that he might have been guilty of giving into temptation, as I sat there in the court room I became increasingly convinced that he was, in fact, totally innocent. There were five witnesses, including Linda Davidson, who persisted in their accusations and were credible witnesses. There were two women who Mr. Grant was able to show as being unsure and uncertain what in fact had transpired in the consulting room and who admitted that it was possible that Tony had legitimately conducted a physical examination and treated minor skin irritations exactly as a competent and diligent physician should have done. And there was Mr. Grant's cross-examination of Mrs. Fernandez which looked very good for us.

Thus, as the days went on, the cumulative effect of Mr. Grant's cross-examinations was to cast some doubt on every witness's testimony. Maybe some of the women weren't ready to admit that they'd made a mistake, and had gotten caught up in the hysteria of the 'rush to judgment,' as the newspapers said, but they were mistaken all the same. At least, that's what I was feeling. Shirley agreed with my sense of things when I'd share it all with her every evening. But, Laura . . . I don't know; I got the impression that Laura was afraid to think positively, afraid to hope or believe. It was as if she'd already decided that Tony would be found guilty and was afraid to hope for anything to the contrary. She was sure that he'd be found guilty and sent to Camp Hill State Prison. Laura was not really receptive to any hopefulness that I expressed.

On the other hand, I have to admit that when the prosecutor, Mr. Sullivan, was presenting his case and leading his witnesses through their testimonies, I didn't feel so confident. He was good. His large imposing frame, his deep syrupy voice, was impressive and filled with an air of authority. In contrast, poor Mr. Grant looked like a boy scout sent to do a man's job. Every once in a while I'd look over at Laura and realize that it might not be a good idea for me to get my hopes up too high. Especially when he had Mrs. Peterson on the stand. She testified that Dr. Cappeletti talked her into letting him do an internal examination. "He told me that if I went to a specialist, that I would be charged more money, but that he could include it in his regular examination. So I let him do it. I've had many pelvic examinations in my life. After all, I'm in my mid-forties and I've had three children. So, I know what to expect. I have to say, I've never had an internal examination like that before."

"Please tell us, Mrs. Peterson, how this exam differed from previous examinations you've had before from qualified gynecologists."

"Well, the internal itself wasn't that different. I mean, he put in the speculum or whatever you call that instrument they use, and he looked inside. It was everything else after that. For example, when he examined my breasts, he stood behind me and reached around to my breasts with both hands and, I don't know, but it sure didn't feel like he was looking for lumps the way he was squeezing them and running his hands back and forth over them. I can tell you, I felt quite uncomfortable."

"Yes, of course. It seemed to you that he was getting some pleasure out of feeling your breasts?"

"Absolutely. His head was right next to mine and he was breathing heavily."

"And how did that make you feel?"

"I was shocked. And a little frightened. I'd been seeing Dr. Cappeletti for a couple of years. My husband went to him and I brought my children, too. I had always had the highest respect for him, so I was shocked and I was thinking: What's going on here? Has he lost his marbles? I was afraid of what he might do."

"And did Dr. Cappeletti in fact do anything else that upset you?"

"Yes, he did. After he did the internal examination and removed that instrument, he spent an inordinate amount of time examining my vagina. I mean the outer part, not the inner part."

"What do you think he was doing all that time?"

"Actually, I asked him, because he was frowning as he was fiddling around down there and I asked him if there was anything wrong. Why was he spending so much time?"

"And how did he respond, Mrs. Peterson. How did he explain himself?"

"He said that I had some inflammation there and that he was putting some Bacitracin on it. He suggested that I make a special effort to keep it clean and to put some ointment on it if I noticed any further inflammation in the future."

"And what was your reaction to that explanation?"

"Why I was totally surprised. I mean, I had never noticed any inflammation before and I'm a very clean person. I take pride in my cleanliness. For him to suggest that I wasn't keeping myself clean enough, well, it just didn't make any sense to me."

"So you didn't believe him."

"No sir, I did not. Not for one minute."

"So you don't believe that you had any genital inflammation at all?"

"Absolutely not."

"Therefore, Dr. Cappeletti must have had some other motivation for spending a good deal of time 'fiddling around down there,' as you said."

"Yes, it seems obvious. At the time, I didn't want to think about it. I couldn't accept what he'd said, but it was too upsetting and I didn't want to think about it right then. But, after I got home, I realized what he'd been doing and I decided right then and there that none of my family, not me, not my husband, and not any of my kids, were ever going to go back to that office again. No sir."

Mr. Grant did his best in his cross-examination, but he couldn't shake her testimony or the passion of her belief. When he went over her testimony with her and tried to suggest that perhaps she might have misinterpreted Tony's actions, she erupted: "No sir. Now you wait a minute. I was there. I know what happened to me. I know what he did to me. Don't you go saying I don't know what happened, because I do. I know what he did."

I'll tell you the truth, she made me wonder. I wanted to believe that she had misinterpreted Tony's behavior and was too defensive about having been told that she had some minor inflammation, but there was no doubting the fact that it looked like she believed what she said. So, yeah, there were times when it was pretty difficult to keep my hopes up.

Casey

Mom and Dad didn't allow any of us kids to go to the trial and refused to discuss it with us. Newspapers were not allowed into the house. But, we go to school. We go downtown. We go to the library. We have access to computers and getting online. So, even though we don't discuss it as a family, I keep pretty much up-to-date. And, as a result, I'm more confused than ever. In the beginning, I didn't want my father to be guilty, but I was afraid he was. Then, I thought that he probably was guilty after all, but that that was okay. But, after reading about the trial, I'm not sure. Some of the articles imply that he's a terrible monster and question what other crimes he may have committed and will other victims come forward? Those articles really make me feel creepy. Sometimes I have the fleeting thought that I'll just cut off my dick and then no one will ever be able to accuse me of anything. But, that thought really scares me because I'm afraid that I might actually do it.

But, then there are other articles that suggest that some of these women may very well be mistaken and victims, not of my father, but of a kind of hysteria. There seems to be a wide-spread fear involving all sorts of sex crimes, especially child sexual abuse. Nobody trusts anybody. Priests are molesting kids, forcing them to give them blow-jobs. Christ! I mean, priests? And teachers having affairs with students. And all these parents hovering over their kids in the parks, in sand boxes and T-ball games, afraid that their kids are going to be kidnapped. Jesus, people are even afraid to leave their dogs alone for fear they'll be dog-napped. It's a crazy world we live in. So, I don't know. I just don't know. I'm hoping that my dad will be found not-guilty, but that might be too much to hope for. I'm thinking that when this is all over, one way or another, we'll probably move. Maybe I'll go into the service when

I'm eighteen and finished with high school, just to get away from everything. That's all I want right now, to just get away from it all.

Jennifer

Things are getting worse at home. Grandma stopped having any alcohol in the house because she thinks Daddy has started drinking too much. All he does is watch TV or sit outside on Grandma's back porch and watch the grass grow. Mom got a job at the hospital in the admissions office in the evenings, so I hardly see her. She's at the trial during the day with Grandpa and then almost immediately goes to St. Ignatius. The house is still and stifling, like a funeral parlor. Even Casey won't talk to me. Grandma sends Mia over to her friends' houses to play because it's so gloomy and edgy here at home.

I go online to see what's happening at the trial because no one here will talk about it. I get the impression that some of the testimony against him has been very damaging so I suppose he will go to prison. The only question is for how long. I just want to know how I can get away from here and put all of this shame behind me. I don't feel like I have a family any more. Nobody is here. Even if they're here, they're not here, you know what I mean? They all are locked up inside themselves. Even Grandma. It's like we're already sealed inside our own individual cells. I'd run away but where would I go? How would I live? If you give me an answer to that, I'll be out of here in a flash. Believe it.

Tony

Tommy presented the last of our witnesses for the defense today, mostly character witnesses. He put on a few women patients who I'd been treating for years to testify how ethical and caring and professional I was. Sally and Bridget testified as to my competence and confirmed how highly regarded I was by my patients. More importantly, they testified that I ran a busy office and hardly ever spent more than ten or fifteen minutes with a patient unless it was something extraordinary, the point being that I did not linger in the examining rooms with female patients. They also testified that they had never heard a word of complaint, either from a patient in the office or in the form of gossip outside the office.

When my father took the stand, he talked about how I had been a boy scout and an alter boy and had always wanted to be a physician because I wanted to help people. Dad did a nice job. He was upset, having to testify, so he made a very sympathetic witness. Tommy was adamant that I not testify on my own behalf, that Sullivan would love to have the opportunity to make me look bad; worse than bad: guilty.

So, tomorrow, Friday, Tommy and Mr. Sullivan will make their closing arguments and then we'll see. Guilty as charged on all accounts or not guilty as charged on all sexual felony accounts and multiple misdemeanors? Or will it be guilty on some charges and not guilty on some others? That bitch, Linda Davidson, was brutal in her testimony against me. I have to hand it to Billy Cobb; he did a great job of setting me up. A little bit of overkill, maybe. He didn't have to totally fucking destroy me in order to tarnish my testimony against him in that wrongful death suit—which, by the way—was dropped because of my predicament; because I was the victim's physician as well as the physician to the county jail. Without me, the plaintiffs had no case.

And Sheila Peterson also cooked my goose. I guess she was the biggest surprise. I had wondered why she and her family had stopped coming to the office, but she'd never said anything. I usually try to make a little conversation when I'm doing a physical exam; you know, make some joke, talk about the news or gossip, just as a way of distracting them from something that might be making them embarrassed or uncomfortable in some way. So, when Sheila stopped coming, I wondered if I'd said something that might have offended her. I know she can be a little uptight sometimes. But, to have her come out with that testimony with such certainty, such angry conviction, it took me totally by surprise. I still don't understand how a patient of mine could actually bring herself to believe that I could have done something like that. I still can't comprehend it. It's so alien, so preposterous, that I can't take it in. It doesn't compute.

I'm sure that the jury won't be meeting over the weekend. So, we've got next week to look forward to. I'm trying to wrap everything up at home because, even if I get off on some of the charges—and I'll always be grateful to Tommy for all that he's done on my behalf—I'm sure that I'll have to go to prison for some of them. I know I'll probably be in there for a good long time. Even if I'm still alive at the end of my sentence, when I come out, what will I have to look forward to? My dad will have passed away by then. He's sixty-six now. Laura and I will be divorced. I don't have any illusions about that, not with the way things have been going lately. And my kids? What kind of relationship will I have with them after twenty or thirty or more years in prison? No, I will have nothing. Nada. Zero. I'd be better off dead. I mean, why go through all those years of hell? For what? I've got nothing to look forward to. Looking back, I don't even know why I bothered going through the trial. For what? To prove I was innocent? Ha! Fat chance I had. I should have known it was futile. Who was it? Betty? Said I was Don Quixote, tilting at windmills. Well, maybe I was. Maybe I was. No wonder Lenny and Bernie bowed out. Bastards. If I'd known at the beginning of all this how it would turn out, losing everything, depriving my family of everything, then maybe I would have put an end to it right then. All this wasted money. All this pain and anguish, for everyone. It's not worth it. It wasn't worth it. It's all so goddamned unfair, so fucking unfair. I don't deserve this.

Betty

Laura came home today and told me that both the prosecution and the defense had presented their closing summaries and that it had gone to the jury. They're meeting now and, assuming they don't reach a decision tonight—and I don't see how they could—they will recess for the weekend and then they'll be back at it on Monday morning. So this is it. Show time. One way or another, this time next week it'll all be over. Finally. Thank God. I can't tell you what a hell it's been on everyone in this house. Tony has taken to drinking. I don't know where he gets the money for it. I know I stopped keeping any liquor around the house because of him. But, in the evening, I can smell it on his breath. Fortunately, for me at least, he spends a lot of time sitting alone on the back porch encased in solitude, sulking and feeling sorry for himself. The ones I feel sorry for are his kids and Laura. I'm hoping that when this is all over, whatever happens, she'll divorce him and get on with her life. What kind of a life could she have with him now, even if he were acquitted? I know that I can't wait for him to be out of this house. Personally, I don't care if he's in prison or hiding out in a rooming house under an alias. I just want to be free of him. I'm tired of that angry morose look and the tension. Christ, the tension is killing me. He's so sensitive, you can't say anything. You don't dare look at him cross-eyed or raise your voice, or even question him. I need some peace and quiet. I'm old enough. I deserve it. I'm too old for all this crap.

Tony

"Well, I'm sorry, Betty, for all the inconvenience I've put you all through. I'm really sorry that you had to put up with some inconvenience and some social embarrassment, but it wasn't exactly my fault, you know."

Betty
"No? Then whose fault was it? Mine? Laura's? Your children's?"

Tony
"Don't be ridiculous. It was Billy Cobb. He brought this all down on us, all of us."

Betty
"He couldn't have done it without your help, sweetheart."

Tony

"What are you talking about? I didn't do anything."

Laura

"Right. You didn't do anything. You didn't bother to have a nurse in the examining room with you when you did pelvic exams."

Tony

"We've been over that."

Laura

"It still doesn't make it right. If you had followed the correct office procedures, if you'd been more professional, then Cobb couldn't have done anything to you."

Tony

"And if I'd hired another nurse, we wouldn't have had the house we had."

Laura

"Had. Where is it now?"

Betty

"Yeah, big spender, where is it now? And the membership to the golf club? And the Mercedes?

Jennifer

"And my college, Dad. Where is the tuition money you were saving?"

Tony

"Go ahead, gang up on me. All right, maybe it didn't work out like I planned. Maybe we've lost everything . . ."

Casey

"Maybe?"

Betty

"No maybe, baby. It all went bye-bye. Kaput."

Tony

"All right. It's all gone, all of it. Everything we had or almost had or ever dreamed of having. It's all gone. But, for a while, we had it. We had the house on Ridge Road, the swimming pool, the private schools, the vacation trips. We had it because I got it for you. And, I wasn't the one who took it away. That's not my doing. Even if I had hired a nurse to be with me and we didn't have the house and everything else, Billy Cobb still would have found a way to bring me down. He'd still have done something to discredit me and to save his own ass. Who knows what he might have done?"

Laura

"It wasn't the sheriff who made you decide to go through with this trial and refuse the plea bargain."

Tony

"I know. I'm sorry. For that, I apologize to all of you. I know now that I was foolish. It was stupid of me to have thought that, somehow, I could have convinced anybody of my innocence. I was naïve and stupid. I thought I was doing the right thing, but now that it's all over, I see that it was a terrible mistake. I admit it. Even though I hadn't done anything wrong and had nothing to feel ashamed of, I should have pleaded guilty to the misdemeanor, lied to the judge and said that I'd exposed myself to that bitch, Fernandez, and taken the thirteen months. I know. I've put all of you through weeks of unnecessary anguish and for nothing. I know they'll probably find me guilty of something. I'm not stupid. Between Linda Davidson and Sheila Peterson, maybe one or two more, I know I won't get off completely. I see that now. But, back then, I thought I was making the right decision. I thought we could convince them. I'm sorry."

Jennifer
"I still love you, Dad."

Tony
"Thanks, sweetie. I love you too. I always will."

Betty, Al, Shirley, Laura, Casey, and Jennifer
"But it's too late baby, now it's too late
Though we really did try to make it
Something inside has died and I can't hide it
And I just can't fake it"[2]

Al
"Tony, listen to me."

Tony
"Huh?"

Al
"I said we all love you. That's never going to change. No matter what happens next week with the jury, whatever they decide, we're always going to love you."

Tony
"I let you down, Pop. You and Mom. All of you."

Jennifer
"Dad, I'd just like to know . . . the things these ladies said . . ."

---

[2]   Song: "Just Can't Fake It." Lyrics and music by Toni Stern and Carole King.

Tony

"Jenn, how can you even ask?"

Laura

"Okay, let's not start that again. You say you didn't do anything. Okay; you didn't do anything. All right? Whatever happened or didn't happen is no longer the issue . . ."

Tony

"Bullshit, Laura. It's everything. Everything! What you believe about me is everything. Don't you see that? Unless you believe in me, all of you, then I don't exist. Ah, fuck it. It's over. It's finished.

Al

"What do you mean, Tony? What's over? What's finished?"

Tony

"Everything, Pop. Everything. My life. It's over. Your anguish, your shame, the embarrassment I've brought to you, to all of you. It's all over now. Next week the jury will come in with their verdict and whatever it is, even if they say 'not guilty' to all of the charges, every one. It's still over. I no longer belong here. I might as well be dead. Gone, one way or another."

Al

"Tony, don't say that."

Laura

"Tony . . ."

Tony

"No, it's true. This whole past year and a half, whatever, this purgatory that we've all been living in; we've all been waiting for judgment day, for the guillotine to fall. Well, judgment day is here, or it will be soon, and the guillotine is about to fall. And, swoosh, I'll be gone.

Jennifer and Casey

"Dad . . ."

Tony

"No, from here on out, I go it alone. You kids, all of you, you'll be better off. Just get on with your lives. Be happy."

Betty

"Feeling sorry for himself again."

Tony

"Fuck you, Betty. I've got a right. Who else is going to feel sorry for me? You? You'll be glad when I'm gone."

Betty

"I won't deny it."

Al

"Betty!"

Betty

"I'm sorry, Al, but it's true. The way your son has been moping around here, hiding out in the dark like he was some goddamned vampire, turning into a lush. He's right, he's already dead in his own mind."

Tony

"Like I said, it's over, all over."

Betty

And that's when he walked out of the house and left us all wondering what he meant. We heard him get into the van and drive away. My first thought was that he went to get something to drink. Laura told me later that she figured that he went up to

Fairfax Mountain to think and calm down. It was natural, she said, for him to be upset and scared, and we probably hadn't been as supportive or as understanding as we might have been. Al and Shirley left and went back to their house. They gave me and Laura and each of the kids a big hug. I could feel Al's body trembling against mine, he was close to sobbing. I think they expected Tony to come back soon or maybe show up at their house. I think that Al was hoping for that. The kids went to their rooms. But later when it got dark and Tony hadn't returned home we began to worry. I assumed he was somewhere, probably half in the bag, feeling sorry for himself. Laura was worried, though, and when the kids came down for supper and he wasn't there, they began to worry too. And by the next morning, I had joined them. Laura called Shirley, but they hadn't seen or heard from him. He'd disappeared. None of us said anything; maybe because we all felt a little guilty. Maybe it's what we wanted, for him to simply walk out of our lives. No fuss, no bother; in a way, just what the doctor ordered.

Monday morning he came back. He apologized for worrying us. The bastard. I know that's what he wanted to accomplish. He said he had to get away and come to terms with everything. Then we went into the kitchen. I made coffee for everybody and we sat down around the table. It was a little awkward, I admit. Mostly we engaged in small talk and drank our coffee, waiting for the telephone call that would tell us that the jury was ready to come in with their verdict.